Rachael was heartbroken at having to leave her lovely old home, Swans' Reach, and she would probably have hated anyone who bought it. But she felt an extra special antipathy to Dominic Retford, with his dark good looks and his air of being monarch of all he surveyed. Never, she said, could they be friends. But she could be wrong . . .

Books you will enjoy
by MARGARET WAY

THE MAN ON HALF-MOON

Katharine's brother Darin had disappeared, somewhere in Queensland, and she could not rest until she had gone up there to see if she could find him. But the problem of Darin's whereabouts paled into insignificance in the face of the much greater problem of how to cope with his boss, the ruthless—and devastatingly attractive—Curt Dangerfield.

FLIGHT INTO YESTERDAY

To Lang Frazer, Natalie was just a spoilt, heartless girl who revelled in hurting her father and her stepmother Britt. But Natalie saw Britt as the woman who had ruined her relationship with her father. How could she see Lang with anything but resentment? What did he know about it all anyway?

RED CLIFFS OF MALPARA

The Merediths had brought Sarie up from childhood, and Blake Meredith had always constituted himself guardian in chief. But now Sarie was beginning to realise that the conflict that had always existed between them was changing into something else. Just what was this new emotion, and how could she deal with it?

A LESSON IN LOVING

Rosslyn was spending the summer vacation at Belyando in Northern Australia, looking after a rather difficult small child—but soon found that her real problems were being caused by the child's uncle, Boyd Ballinger, who announced that he was a bachelor and intended to remain one!

SWANS' REACH

BY

MARGARET WAY

MILLS & BOON LIMITED
17–19 FOLEY STREET
LONDON W1A 1DR

First published 1976
This edition 1977

© Margaret Way 1976

ISBN 0 263 72364 X

*Made and printed in Great Britain by
Richard Clay (The Chaucer Press), Ltd. Bungay, Suffolk*

CHAPTER ONE

RACHAEL sprang to her feet, feeling so threatened that she instinctively seized up a paperweight. 'No, damn him! Why should *he* be so fortunate? I won't have it!'

The dangerous words were out before she realised she had said them—so violent, so irrational, she would have been at a loss to explain them herself, but undoubtedly strong feeling propelled her, illuminating her skin and her eyes, a flame of emotion that she wore like armour, though Jacob's bulk almost hid her slenderness from sight.

A bright fury in a yellow dress! How young and desperate she looks! Elizabeth Ross, who loved her granddaughter, remained silent, but Jacob, their dear friend and solicitor for over forty years, turned brusquely on the girl with a sharp look of pity and censure. 'Put down that paperweight, Rachael. You're upsetting your grandmother!' He was studying her intently. She looked uncannily wild, but somehow beautiful beyond enduring. Such a proud and spirited young thing! It was really very moving. 'Rachael?' His eyes clung to the paperweight until she deposited it safely on the desk again.

'I'm sorry, Uncle Jacob!' Rachael came back to order with an effort, all her bright colour just as suddenly fading. 'You couldn't expect me to be happy. My head is reeling. I don't want it to be *him*. He looks

5

as if he owns the earth already, every last wish fulfilled. If we must sell, why *him*?'

For once Jacob Dodds looked at a loss. He ran his hand over his perfectly bald dome. 'My dear child, be fair! I don't know why you're feeling so badly.'

'Yes, darling, what is it?' Elizabeth Ross spoke for the first time since Rachael's passionate outburst, even in her adoration realising her only grandchild's penchant for drama.

The golden iridescent light was in Rachael's eyes again. She swung around looking momentarily betrayed, and stared fixedly at her grandmother. 'Why, Gran, I haven't a logical explanation. He's too disturbing a man. He makes me anxious, panicky—his whole image. Who does he think he is—Caesar, a tyranniser? Why, his glance would slice you to ribbons. That's his ghastly profession.'

'Good lord!' Jacob, by now, was thoroughly startled. 'May I remind you, Rachael,' he said sternly, 'I, too, practised law.'

'As the head of a firm of highly respected solicitors, Uncle Jacob.'

'While Nick Retford is probably the most brilliant criminal lawyer in the country.'

'Really quite decent after all,' Elizabeth pointed out gently, seeking to influence the atmosphere.

Rachael stared into space. 'I'm not thinking of myself, Gran,' she said tragically. 'Don't you notice? What would a man like that know about feelings?'

'Everything, I should think,' Elizabeth said reasonably.

'I don't believe it! He'd have as much human kind-

6

ness as a tiger. Didn't you see his cleft chin? No soft, easy focus there. I thought he looked quite ruthless.'

'Well, well, well!' Jacob breathed helplessly.

Elizabeth continued to smile—an asset in all situations. 'I thought him a most striking man. Splendid, we would have said in my day. A man to hurdle any challenge, and, as Jacob informs us, he's considered to be extremely brilliant. A good combination, don't you think? I should be proud of him, but I suppose you're too young and headstrong to see these things.'

There was horror in Rachael's young voice as though she was in the middle of a nightmare. 'You couldn't let the Swan go to him, Gran? How brutal! I'll have a nervous breakdown.'

Elizabeth raised her silvery, beautifully dressed head, assuming her own effective tone. 'No exaggeration, darling, my own nerves are at breaking point. Let's face it, our days at Swans' Reach are over and done with. All the old glory passed with the death of your grandfather. The death duties crippled us and we simply haven't the wherewithal to care for such a very large house, let alone the grounds. There's no use making a scene. We must act properly, if not in front of poor old Jacob here who knows us.'

'You're wonderful, Elizabeth,' Jacob said sincerely.

'Well, I'm not going to make myself ill at the prospect of leaving my home, even if it is a great inconvenience and a heartbreak. I shall make my farewells quietly, with dignity. Mr Retford made a very good impression upon me. Apart from the singular fact he's the only one to come up to the reserve price, he's obviously a man of taste and distinction.'

7

'Do you happen to realise how he makes his living, Gran? Defending *murderers*!'

'Don't be ridiculous, child! He's immensely respectable.'

'I think it's downright horrible to be a criminal lawyer,' Rachael announced, almost sobbing. 'Nothing ever turns out the way it should.'

'Darling,' Elizabeth said, looking suddenly very frail, 'we *must* go. You know that. You only met Mr Retford briefly, just as he was leaving. I had a much better opportunity to assess his character.'

'He's Judge Housman's great-nephew, isn't he?' Rachael asked, as though she suddenly remembered something.

'What has that got to do with it?' Jacob asked blankly.

'Sir Geoffrey was madly in love with Gran for years.'

'My dear girl, he wasn't the only one. I was, still am, myself.'

'Of course, Jacob, how nice you are!'

'She's like you when you were young, Lib. The same beautiful hair, the same topaz eyes with a slant to them, but she doesn't have your sweet temperament, those soft, disarming ways.'

'No,' Elizabeth smiled. 'She's Dirk's daughter. Such a passion for life he had, my beloved son. Rachael is my greatest link with his memory. I can't ever be angry with her.'

'I love you too, Gran,' Rachael said emotionally, 'but selling Swans' Reach to Dominic Retford is out of the question. He might turn it into some kind of

8

reform school, a rehabilitation centre for all his old clients.'

'I shouldn't worry my head about that, darling. I believe he's thinking of marrying again. The Maybury woman. What's her name?'

'Vanessa,' Jacob supplied, interested on his own account.

'That social butterfly!' Rachael cried scornfully.

'She looks very beautiful in all her photographs,' Lady Ross said fairly.

'Just as cold and remote as a statue. Like *him*. Certainly they should make a congenial pair.'

'Don't be so unkind, Rachael,' Jacob replied. 'I've seen Mrs Maybury. She's an absolute picture and very witty. Retford's had his own troubles. He deserves some happiness. It was a tragedy about his wife.'

'Why, did she leave him?'

'She died of leukemia, I understand. She was only twenty-five and their son was three years old.'

'There!' Rachael drew a breath hoarsely. 'I'm sorry, I'm sorry. I know I sound shocking. What's the matter with me, for heaven's sake?'

'You can't bear leaving your lovely home, that's all,' Jacob said briskly, polishing his glasses. 'It's perfectly understandable. I could weep buckets for you myself, but the halycon days of Swans' Reach haven't fallen into dust. Retford is a man of considerable means.'

'All treasures left to him. Inherited wealth!' Rachael said bitterly. 'I suppose dear old Sir Geoffrey will leave him a packet as well.'

'Why not? He's the Judge's acknowledged heir. Housman never married. To the best of my knowledge the only woman who laid any frail claim to his attention was your grandmother, and she was married.'

'Make another attempt to meet Mr Retford,' Lady Ross said. 'You may see him in a different light.'

'*Never!* He's a confounding kind of man face to face.'

'Well, he's coming again the day after tomorrow.'

'And to think our home could go to a man like that!'

Elizabeth ran a trembling hand across her forehead, but her voice was quite firm. 'You're going to listen to me, Rachael. It's not really sensible to allow yourself to become violently prejudiced against a man on the basis of a half dozen exchanged words. You can't really know a thing about him.'

'I'd have known all about him if I met him in the middle of the Gobi desert.'

'How wrongly you judge him! I seem to have seen the exact opposite.'

'You're like a nun, Gran. Blind to the wickedness around you.'

'Don't bother to spare me!'

'Your grandmother, Rachael, is a very balanced woman,' Jacob said testily. 'She's even considered to be very worldly.'

'Not by me.'

'And how do I appear to myself?' Elizabeth asked with a little laugh. 'Poor Mr Retford, so unsuspecting of all this passion and hatred.'

'He knew very well I didn't like him,' Rachael said. 'Didn't you notice his eyes, Gran? Such a theatrical combination, black hair and blue eyes.'

'Red hair has a few drawbacks as well,' Jacob pointed out drily.

'Dark auburn,' Rachael corrected.

'Until you get under a light, darling, then it flashes out all the red in the world. Don't worry, it's beautiful hair, as you very well know. You were extremely lucky to have inherited it from me. Your dearest grandfather lost his hair quite early.'

'Oh, Gran! What about the Lodge? Did you say anything about that to him?'

'No, actually I didn't,' Lady Ross replied carefully.

'Why not?'

'Darling, I'm not begging for anything.'

'The house stands on ten acres,' Rachael said heatedly. 'Surely he can let us have the Lodge and the bit of ground round it?'

'Such a proposition mightn't appeal to him, let alone his future wife. It would mean subdividing the estate.'

'Perhaps he might consider leasing it to you, Lib? It seems the ideal situation to me. I can't see you cooped up in an apartment after all this. It's just big enough and most beautifully furnished. You could keep all those pieces.'

'Mr Retford mightn't want us on his doorstep, Jacob dear.'

'Damn his eyes!' Rachael said violently.

'The eyes got you, didn't they, darling? A very *vivid* blue, as I recall.'

'I'm sure Lucifer had blue eyes.'

'There's a thing!'

'Blue is the most arrogant colour in the world,' Rachael insisted.

11

'What you took for arrogance, my darling, was just a naturally commanding presence. You over-reacted.'

'As usual. Say it, Gran.'

'Truly, I've spoilt you. So did Lew. We spoilt you outrageously—not that you haven't always been the dearest girl in the world. Your good points far out-weigh your hot temper. Meet him again, darling.'

'I suppose I'll doubly detest him.'

'Don't make a mischief, there's a dear girl,' Jacob said persuasively. 'Nick Retford is our greatest bet so far. You didn't meet the big real estate developer. Now *that* would have been impossible.'

'You never told me about him, Gran.'

'It wasn't worth it. A very ill-bred man, absolutely no cultivated instincts. If I must sell Swans' Reach, it will go to a man I can trust with it. As I see it, Dominic Retford.'

'How *could* you, Gran?' sighed Rachael.

'I'm wiser than you are, darling. You talk a good deal of nonsense. But your heart's in the right place, and you're desperately lovely, even if I say so myself. None of your friends' mothers will. I can honestly say being good-looking counts with a woman. A man doesn't seem to be any the worse off if he's ugly.'

'Thank God for that!' Jacob said gratefully.

'I wish I were a man!' Rachael said vehemently.

'Horror of horrors!' Lady Ross threw up her hands, smiling.

'Then we wouldn't have to sell the Swan, Gran!' Rachael looked at her grandmother with her heart in her eyes. 'I'd work like a slave!'

'Darling, even you couldn't make a fortune by

12

twenty, even though I've devoted a good deal of time to your education.'

'You're the best and most unselfish grandmother in the world.'

'Hear, hear!' said Jacob fondly.

'Then have pity on me, darling. Try and hide your aversion to our most interested and well-heeled buyer. I understand he's bringing Mrs Maybury next time.'

'I hope she ruins him!' Rachael couldn't resist saying.

'I don't think he's the man to give in to a woman's whims and fancies. It's just possible Mrs Maybury might be extremely virtuous.'

'Then she'll make him an odd wife. I think he'd be a demon in the courtroom, and to prove it, I just might go and see him tomorrow in action. Isn't he defending that Cleary boy?'

'Rachael!' Lady Ross turned about in the Louis XVI settee. 'You must be mad! What need have you to do that?'

'I want to see for myself what kind of a man he is,' Rachael said very imperiously.

For all their closeness Lady Ross looked appalled.

'The experience won't hurt her,' Jacob found himself saying. 'One must take the opportunities life has to offer. The closing stages of the trial, as it happens. I expect the boy will get off. An unstable type perhaps, but not, I think, a murderer.'

'He should be very grateful he has Mr Retford to defend him,' Rachael said caustically.

'A good thing indeed. I wouldn't like an innocent boy to end up in prison.'

13

Rachael took that without flinching, continuing to meet Jacob's shrewd old eyes. She was very fond of him, so after a minute she smiled, unaware that her smile was, and always would be, heart-stopping, but for the moment Jacob had to discount it. 'It might be awkward if Retford sees you.'

'He won't,' Rachael announced confidently. 'I'll wear a hat.'

'Excuse me, darling,' her grandmother said gently, 'but I don't believe you have one.'

'I'll wear one of yours.'

'Then he'll certainly see you,' Lady Ross answered, affronted. 'Mine were made to be noticeable. What's the sense of a hat one might miss? I'd feel quite disabled without a beautiful hat.'

'It's all right, Gran. We allow for you,' Rachael said with a pert grin.

'All you young girls are so keen on this unisex thing, it's a wonder anyone wants to marry you.'

'In view of the evidence Rachael presents to us, that won't be her problem,' Jacob said gallantly.

'I'm saving myself for the right man and I've plenty of time to spare. It's even possible I mightn't marry at all.'

'How disquieting,' her grandmother said smoothly. 'And I suppose you're determined to go along to-morrow.'

'Want to come?'

'Heavens, no! I'm not even acquainted with the case. I can't see the necessity for all this ugliness all over the papers. There's not a great deal else to read these days.'

14

'I bet he's very expensive,' said Rachael as though accusing Dominic Retford of something.

'I should say so,' Jacob observed thoughtfully, 'but he's probably the best counsel at the Bar. Certainly way ahead of all the younger men. He's worth every penny. I think he's won every case he's been briefed for.'

'He's certainly very sure of himself, and those penetrating eyes!'

'Well, I must away,' Jacob said. 'I'm very busy.'

'Let me come down to the car with you, Uncle Jacob.'

'There's a good girl. Go and fetch my things.'

When Rachael had gone out of the room, Elizabeth and Jacob looked at each other. 'Take courage, my dear.' Jacob reached out and patted Elizabeth's shoulder. 'I'll always be standing by to help you.'

'You're a good friend, Jacob!' She covered his hand with her own, firming the little tremor in her voice.

'Think nothing of it. I welcome the opportunity. Though none can see it, I know of your grief, Libby. I'm very proud of you. Lew would be too.'

'I must try to forget Swans' Reach. That I ever came to it as a bride. That my only son was born here. That my dearest Lewis loved it so well and died peacefully in his own garden. It's been a long journey for me too. I'll be eighty next birthday. I haven't got much longer. My heart aches for Rachael. It's her turn now and she's so vulnerable—she needs protection. Even the fact of her beauty. In many ways she's a *young* twenty. Her friend Sally might be double her age!'

'I know what you mean.' Even Jacob had to sigh.

'But you can be very proud of her, Lib. There's real quality there. Perhaps a shade too much fire, these young things! It's a natural reaction, this sudden vehemence towards Retford. She'll give way and adopt a more sensible attitude. And she loves you so well she'll do anything to put your mind at rest.'

Elizabeth allowed herself to be helped to her feet, leaning a little against her friend. Jacob was indeed a tower of strength. 'When Rachael develops such a dislike, there might be the devil to pay!'

Jacob looked down at her thoughtfully. Such a wonderful-looking woman, still, with her beautiful, glowing hair gone snow white and her skin like a fine rose petal. 'Now see here, Lib,' he said slowly. 'In spite of Rachael's youth and her sheltered upbringing, she doesn't make any mistakes. She's always been a credit to her honoured name. She did wonderfully well in her exams and she works hard. This little emotional outburst will pass. The only masculine authority she's ever known was Lew's, and God knows he was her devoted slave from the day she was born. Her dear father she scarcely knew. Nick Retford must have challenged some secret part of her, her deepest femininity. Such a lively girl would naturally tend to be self-willed. I'm not disturbing you, am I, dear?'

'No, no, Jacob. You're my true friend. To all appearances Mr Retford seemed greatly taken with the place.'

'Well, it's no humble abode after all!' Jacob said drily. 'I've never been in a more beautiful house. I wish there was some way I could save it for you. To lose Swans' Reach at your age! A whole world of

16

regret. These death duties simply must be abolished. They're affecting everyone, not only the rich, but the middle and lower income brackets. Harry is handling the Clayton estate. Dear me, difficulties there! Such a pity!'

Lady Ross only shrugged. 'They'll change it in due time, Jacob, but it won't help me. I must leave my peace and my haven, but I mustn't complain. I've been very fortunate, after all. Life took my only child from me in his prime, and our dear Marianne, but somehow Lew and I survived. Rachael pulled us through that double tragedy. There was always the child to consider and she brought us great joy. My little Rachael, she feels this dreadfully. You know how attached she is to the house!'

'She hasn't lost everything, Lib. She's a beautiful girl, well educated, and I don't think she'll be frightened of standing on her own feet. It would be too bad if there was nothing, but you'll still be comfortably off. A paradise like this demands a good deal of time and money. If Retford doesn't have the time he certainly has the necessary means to maintain such a very beautiful home. Rachael, poor child, can't see that he's actually a very desirable person on all counts. Mrs Maybury, I believe, is a brilliant hostess.'

'Well, that doesn't profoundly move me, Jacob.'

'I'm sorry, my dear! I'm a tactless old fool. Always have been.'

'Nonsense, Jacob! You could have been a career diplomat. Ah, here's Rachael.'

Rachael came towards them, a dazzling young creature indeed, making a business of carrying Jacob's packed briefcase. 'What do you keep in here, Uncle Jacob?'

'A novel, my dear. A magnificent first novel!'

'You're joking!' Lady Ross turned to her friend, astonished.

'Why not? There's many a story he could tell!' Rachael said slyly.

Jacob flung up his hands and gave his rich, infectious laugh. 'No, actually, it's an immense amount of work, otherwise I should stay for luncheon.'

'But you've retired, Jacob.'

'Nonsense!' Jacob said jauntily. 'I'm still the up and coming man. Now give me that briefcase, Rachael.' He ambled to the door, a ponderous, impressive figure flanked by the two very slender women. 'Still determined to go and see our friend Mr Retford?'

'I won't be able to help myself,' Rachael said drily. 'It's a kind of compulsion.'

'Just see you don't provoke a crisis.'

'I promise, Uncle Jacob. I'll stay very much in the background.'

'Not with that face! Still, perhaps it's right that you should see him in his own sphere.' Jacob turned a little awkwardly to his life-long friend. 'Goodbye, Lib my dear. I'll ring you tonight, shall I? Rachael can come down to the car with me.'

'And why can't I?' Lady Ross demanded, as though she could see the curtain coming down on her powers.

'Because I won't let you,' Jacob said easily. 'You look marvellous, as always, but perhaps a little tired.'

'I agree with Uncle Jacob,' Rachael said instantly.

'I like you better when you don't. I'm not in the least tired, either of you!'

'Well, you know what we mean!' Jacob waddled a little way off. 'It's natural for ladies to put their feet up.'

'I've spent my entire life keeping busy, thank you, Jacob Dodds. Put my feet up indeed! Give my love to Harry. We don't see nearly enough of him these days. His godmother too!'

'Neither do I, and I'm his father!' Jacob protested, looking down his large fine nose. 'Harry works much too hard, but all Sonia's extravagances have to be paid for.'

'These society women!' Rachael cried, plunging right in. 'Sonia would know Mrs Maybury!'

'I shouldn't wonder,' Jacob said lugubriously. 'Now come along, Rachael, you'll get no more out of me.'

'Not even a ride down to the front gate? It's not every day I can do that in a Daimler.'

'Ask yourself how many other women either?' Lady Ross said waspishly. 'Goodbye, Jacob dear. Stay for lunch next time. In an hour, Rachael, may I remind you. A beautiful day seems to slow you down.'

'I'll be back, Gran. It's heartless to separate us from Swans' Reach. I shall start saying goodbye to it.'

Her grandmother nodded. 'We'll get used to it,' she said with asperity, but little waves of cold shock were radiating out from her heart. It was a good thing in many ways she hadn't much time left for sadness or nostalgia.

Jacob saluted her brisky, looking incredibly near

tears, then he took hold of Rachael's elbow, propelling her down the short flight of white marble steps. His heavy jaw was clenched and there was a tremble under his iron grasp. 'Dear, dear, dear!' he said all the while.

'Some people would commit suicide if they had to leave here!' Rachael said, very nearly sobbing herself.

'I thought I had explained to you, Rachael. You mustn't upset your grandmother. God knows she's desperately trying to cope with all this herself.'

Rachael threw back her head, the sun flashing out all its glorious shades of red. 'Don't worry. I'll behave. Nothing is more important than Gran, but I can't keep it all to myself, Uncle Jacob. You're the nearest thing to family I have. If it were anyone but *that* man. Dear, sweet heaven!'

'Use your head, Rachael!' Jacob said almost violently for him. 'Not your volatile emotions. For heaven's sake, the man isn't an outsider, he's one of us.'

'It's my duty to tell you, Uncle Jacob, you're a snob.'

'Yes, I am! You know what I mean. He will fit very neatly into all this.'

'There's something he'll have to contend with,' Rachael said heatedly. 'I hate him already!'

'A pity, because he's going to get Swans' Reach, mark my words.'

'Yes!' Rachael's golden eyes glittered. 'Life would be simple for a man like that. A man of stature, strong and ruthless.'

'Oh, Rachael, Rachael!' Jacob moaned. 'If I told you he's anything but, you wouldn't believe me. Nick Retford is held in the very highest regard by his peers.'

'Not so fantastic if he wins all his cases.'

'Well, I can do nothing about it, Rachael. You'll make everything so much worse if you don't try to be sane about all this. We don't want Mr Retford to slip through our fingers. Money's tight, and he's prepared to come up to an outstanding figure. You know whatever you do and say affects your grandmother.'

'So what do you want me to do, Uncle Jacob?'

'Be nice to Mr Retford.'

'Mr Retford be damned!' Rachael cried, pain and resentment bursting from her heart. Then she caught sight of Jacob's face and abruptly subsided. 'Oh, all right, if it helps any, I'll smile at him.'

Jacob laughed aloud. 'The sudden shock might be too much for his system. You were very fiery and scornful the other day.'

'So you noticed?' Rachael asked, much surprised.

'As did Mr Retford,' Jacob pointed out with his most judicial expression. 'He's not the man to miss anything.'

'Well, he'll just have to content himself with the house. You can't win 'em all!'

'Your grandmother liked him,' Jacob pointed out.

Rachael swished past him, quite scandalised. 'Gran is susceptible to personalities. Can I drive?'

'No.'

She opened the passenger door and slid in. 'No doubt Mr Retford made it his business to be charming.'

Jacob shut the door on her, peering in at her lovely vivid face. 'I didn't think you'd grant him any such thing.'

'As far as I'm concerned he's corrosive, but yes, I

can see a lot of women might find him ... *interesting*.'

'How grudging!' Jacob trudged around to the other side of the black, gleaming vehicle. 'A man as brilliant as Nick Retford has no right to be interesting to women as well, but I quite agree with you, he's the kind women leap at.'

'I never said that.'

'I'm telling you something important all the same.'

'I know my own mind, Uncle Jacob,' Rachael insisted.

'Of course you don't! None of us do to the last day of our lives.'

'I love you.'

'Well, really! I say, do you mean that?'

'Yes, I do.'

'Then I'll leave you my Daimler.'

'I insist you stay around for ever. I don't want anything else.'

Jacob started up the engine and it purred in his face. 'I'll be around when you need me, God willing. Actually I'm a year older than Lib.'

'How old is Gran?' asked Rachael. 'She never would tell me.'

'Then I won't tell you myself!' Jacob said with wry amusement. 'When your grandmother was young, she looked very much like yourself. Don't take any notice of her portrait. It's good enough, but it didn't do her justice. In every respect, let me tell you, Elizabeth was quite outstanding. I couldn't tell you the number of broken hearts when she accepted old Lew. I had to keep as far away as I could until after Dirk was born, otherwise I would have broken down and cried like a schoolboy. I loved her madly. Ah, there's the front gate now.'

'What about Judge Housman?'

'Oh, he was bowled over by her as well! Got very sour and disgusted afterwards. Anyway, he got ahead. It was tough on my wife, the dearest, best wife in the world, but she knew.'

'Heavens!' said Rachael, in her turn surprised. 'That must have been difficult for her, her husband preferring someone else.'

'The majority of men do that!'

'Really, Uncle Jacob!'

'You forget how many divorces I've dealt with. Don't blame me. Blame human nature. It applies to the wives as well. Most of them have confessed to wanting to strangle their husbands.'

Rachael gurgled in her throat, her face brightening at Jacob's expression. 'Let me down here. I'm going to walk back slowly. Mrs Maybury's husband, was he a divorce client of yours?'

'No, actually, he died. She's a widow.'

'And now to be chained to Mr Retford.'

'I believe she's very enthusiastic about it.'

'I don't in the least care,' shrugged Rachael.

'Deep down in your heart?' Jacob inquired.

Rachael got out of the car, her cheeks burning, 'Please, Uncle Jacob, *believe* me!'

'You really think he's as bad as that?'

'I thought he was perfectly horrible!'

'Then forgive me for being a crazy old fool!' Jacob smiled and waved his hand. 'See you, my dear, don't let your lunch get cold!'

'Now you're teasing. It's only ham salad.'

'Swear you'll behave yourself tomorrow.'

'I'll just be a poor creature, admiring.'

'You'll find a court of law very sobering. A criminal court is always tragic. The boy is lucky he has Retford to defend him. You may be sure he believes in his client's essential innocence.'

'I certainly hope so. I can see him defending the devil and getting him off. No doubt if the devil made a good offer . . .'

'Really, Rachael!' Jacob said repressively, reproach in his face. 'I might have guessed you'd be compelled to say that.'

'Rest easy, Uncle Jacob, I'll do my very best to reconcile myself, if only for Gran's sake.'

'This blow isn't going to prolong her life.'

Rachael brought up her head so sharply she struck it on the car. 'That will be *my* worst blow, Uncle Jacob. I realise I can't have her for ever.'

'I'm not cruelly reminding you of it, my dearest child, it's just that I want you to bear all these things in mind.'

For a moment Rachael was utterly silent, and Jacob saw clearly the vulnerable, defenceless look, of which Elizabeth sometimes spoke. 'There's no doubt in my mind if we all pull together we'll get through this thing with a minimum of trauma. I expect you will come to think the same. A lot depends on you, Rachael. The time is approaching when you must show just how self-sacrificing you can be. I know you're made of real quality.'

24

'Thank you, Uncle Jacob,' she said calmly, 'but only Mr Retford can give the verdict.'

'Smile at him, Rachael, as you promised, and he'll give you anything you want!'

Jacob's glance didn't waver and Rachael was made to feel very conscious of the serious note. She might have been an enchantress with a magic wand, Dominic Retford, in thrall, at her feet. The very idea made her laugh.

'That's an odd way to talk! As though a smile could trap Mr Retford.'

'It's been done before. Take the magnificent Caesar! The haughty and disdainful Mark Antony. Take *me*. No, perhaps you'd better not. Nick Retford, at least, fits the heroic illustrations. All that dark, easy splendour. Wouldn't you say he's a very handsome man?'

'I'd feel a traitor if I did, but yes, he's colourful enough in the grand old tradition. Beyond that, I can't be drawn.'

'Just agree not to quarrel.'

'I'll do it for you, Uncle Jacob. I'll be an angel child with a mission. Not to frighten off the divine Retford.'

'You're going to lead some man a dance.'

'Lots of conflict! I thrive on it.'

'Just because you're jealous of Mrs Maybury!'

'Of *whom*?' Rachael almost shrieked, but Jacob had started up the car again, laughing inordinately at his own penetrating observation. Rachael stood in the drive shaking her fist after him, a gesture he acknowledged with a superior honk of the horn before he disappeared through the huge wrought-iron gates. On an impulse, Rachael ran up and clanged them shut. They were doomed, but for now, she could keep out the world. Nick Retford, his money and power. Damn the man! His impact. She and the Swan belonged together. Her great-great-grandfather had built it in the late 1830s. Captain James Ross had come to the colony of New South Wales in charge of his own ship and a small private fortune in gold sovereigns, and took up this very piece of land, becoming active in colonial politics as did his sons and grandsons. So close to the capital, the original estate had been drastically reduced at the turn of the century to allow for urban development and finally classified as a private residence, with ten very beautiful acres at the heart of the once great property. Swans' Reach was still very valuable, and the homestead an exceptionally fine building in the Regency style, with a colonnaded two-storey central section flanked by single-storey wings. A house with classic white columns and green shuttered windows and a vast sweep of emerald green lawn that ran down to the shining reach of the river just had to be beautiful.

Rachael turned and walked back up the long curving drive. The branches of the beautiful evergreens intermingled, creating a cool greeny-gold grotto. Beyond them lay the parkland studded with every tree and shrub imaginable, planned so there would always be something blooming throughout the year. There were great beds of lush roses, elegantly formal, great freeflowing drifts of azaleas and rhododendrons, the incomparable springtime magic of all Gran's favourite bulbs, the daffodils and freesias and tulips with colours ranging from deepest scarlet to pure white; the great stands of iris, the goddess of the rainbow, beside the reach of the river beloved of the black swans with their snowy white primaries and red bills; the traditional camellia walk, the arbours with climbing roses and wisteria and clematis and the grapevines that yielded a rich harvest for the table; the collection of beautiful garden sculpture that Grandfather Ross had brought back from Italy, the cherubs and nymphs and even a statue of St Francis feeding the birds. The gazebo set under the oak trees and the flower-filled urns of all shapes and sizes, Ali Baba pots, some standing as tall as a man.

I can't bear it! Rachael thought, and suddenly tore through the trees, falling to the scented earth and burying her face in the sweet-smelling grass. Some things should never be expected of one. To sacrifice one's beloved home—it was like cuting off one's right hand. It must be worse for Gran. She turned her head to the reach of the river, her senses drinking in the beauty that was everywhere. She would be helpless without the land. The Swan was protection. It was her life. A beautiful black swan and her fluffy white cygnets sailed in tranquillity over the mirror-like surface of the water. It was impossible not to have tears sting one's eyes.

Rachael followed their progress, such a deeply familiar sight. She loved the swans with every beat of her heart and every throb of her pulse. Their reach of the river was almost a bird sanctuary. Each one of the swans had a name taken from classical mythology, and Gran could charm them right out of the water. Swans'

Reach was splendid and she wasn't going to have it ruled by an usurper. This paradise, this romantic survival from a past age, belonged to a Ross. A malign fate had made possible Dominic Retford's intrusion into their charmed circle. She saw his face clearly in her mind's eye: the chiselled patrician features, the blue, blue eyes. There could be nothing but conflict between them. Losing Swans' Reach to such a man would be an intolerable sacrifice.

For the first time in her life she knew a little about hatred. It was thoroughly uncivilised and she couldn't really understand her attitude herself, but she would have to fight for control every time she met the man. Her beautiful eyes were sparkling like topaz. What was she supposed to do when she was being pulled apart, *smile*? Wasn't he making her wretched enough? On the other hand, a smile could be a lethal instrument. She didn't have it in her heart to show a bit of mercy to Nick Retford. She shut her eyes, but even then she found it difficult to dismiss his image. Tomorrow she would know much more about him. As far as she was concerned Nick Retford was on trial as well.

CHAPTER TWO

RACHAEL knew nothing of a court of law, so she was unprepared for its severity, the enormous difference between the atmosphere of total freedom she was used to and the shocking glimpse into the life of a young man under arrest. Her stomach was tied in knots and her mouth was dry. It was impossible not to become affected by the tension. Impossible not to feel a shaken flame of admiration for the counsel for the defence. He was unquestionably brilliant, everything about him perfect for his chosen profession, streets ahead of the prosecuting counsel, his presence in the courtroom commanding, his voice with a peculiar beauty and clarity, the examinations and cross-examinations, forceful where necessary, powerful, dispassionate, courteous, grave, witty, sarcastic, the numerous clashes with the prosecution seemingly all won. Every eye in the courtroom was fixed upon him whenever he rose to speak and Rachael herself, in the public gallery, became so preoccupied that she ignored the fact that her left foot was developing a cramp.

She was sobered and startled, jolted into harsh reality. A world of suffering, of ugliness, the sordid nightmare moments. Pray God she might never have them, yet tragedy struck everywhere. It happened in families; the rich and the powerful, the comfortable and secure, the poor and oppressed. Murder struck in exclusive circles as well as in slums. This was the other side of life, a dramatic reality, crime and punishment. She felt totally engrossed, her mind sifting every piece of new evidence presented as well as what she had read up in preparation. A queer excitement burned in her. In this day and age she would have thought a man would look a little ridiculous in a wig and gown, but there was Dominic Retford just as striking as a man could be, his blue eyes so lancing one felt he could get anything out of anyone. Certainly the evidence of the last witness for the prosecution had been turned inside out, and had scored appreciably for the defence.

Cleary, the accused, was only a year or so older than Rachael herself. He looked so white and frightened that, guilty or not, Rachael felt a great wave of pity for him. It might well be his last appearance as a free man. The circumstances behind the trial were as old as time. A crime of passion. A brawl over a woman—in this case, Cleary's wife of a few months. There had been an argument at a party, and the young wife had gone home with another man. The facts as brought out by the defence were that neither Cleary nor his wife had met the deceased previously, so there was no premeditated motive for murder. A violent fight had ensued, first in a house and from there to the street, during which the deceased had sustained a fatal head injury. The plea for the defence was manslaughter with extenuating circumstances, but the prosecution had taken and developed the line that Cleary had really intended to kill his young wife's admirer, a man she had become involved with, though so briefly. Cleary at that moment was probably facing a life sentence.

He doesn't look a murderer, Rachael thought. He looked very young and tortured by remorse, but at least he kept his head whenever he was questioned. His wife, who was in the court, kept directing agonised glances towards him, but he never once looked her way. Her testimony confirmed all the evidence her husband had given. She too, it was apparent, was undergoing her own personal hell, a torment from which there was no escape. Whatever happened, whether her husband would be released to her or not, the trial would be a part of them for ever. As long as they both lived. If she was telling the truth, and not motivated by her renewed love and loyalty towards her husband, then the fatal incident had just been a cruel twist of fate, a tragic and needless accident. The deceased had been a strong and hearty young man well able to defend himself. The prosecution had not been able to shake her. The punishment would be in remembering; both of them knew and acknowledged it.

There would be no adjournment. The trial was nearing the end. There was utter silence in the court when Retford stood up. Rachael felt a strange involuntary thrill of confidence in him, and she recognised her own perversity. Some men had an aura of brilliance and authority that could be turned to tremendous advantage, and Dominic Retford was just such a man. No ordinary mortal with that clever alert face, the power and self-assurance that seemed as much a part of him as his black robe and the formal wig, inexplicably right on him, emphasising the polished tan of his skin, the intense blue of his eyes. Perhaps Cleary had really intended to kill his rival, but here was Retford, very lean and tall in his barrister's gown, about to convince all of them, judge, jury, the press, everyone in the public gallery, that his client was guilty of no more than assault under extreme provocation. So much depended on defence counsel, because Cleary now looked in a sick daze, on the point of collapse.

The judge, a famous one, had his head down, making notes. The jury stared fixedly into Retford's face, seemingly rapt, carried along by his reasoning, his utter conviction, for no sense of confusion was allowed. It had all happened just as he was unravelling. When he had finished there was dead silence. The drop of a pen would have come as an explosion. A short pause before the counsel for the prosecution rose to his feet.

Retford shot a rapier glance around the packed courtroom. Searing blue eyes narrowed and rested briefly on Rachael's young face. She felt the shock of it right through to her bones. He couldn't possibly know her. She had skilfully disguised herself in one of Sally's short bubbly dark wigs. It was like wearing a mask. She looked quite different as a brunette—even Gran said so. There was no reason for her to feel this sharp spurt of panic, engulfed by paralysis. She couldn't face this man on a witness stand. He *couldn't* know her, yet the blue gaze, after travelling on, came back to her.

She could feel herself flushing. Feel the wave of heat and shame to her hairline. A moment before she had felt numb, wrung out with tension, but now she was burningly alive. He *did* know her. It didn't seem possible, but that vivid contemptuous gaze conveyed instantly that he recognised her and thought her a silly little fool. The sooner she got away from his hypnotic gaze the better. Besides, she couldn't bear to hear the cold impersonal voice of the prosecuting counsel imputing crime to the most normal human emotions. She couldn't wait to hear the verdict. The tension would be unbearable. She would ache like Cleary, like his young wife, almost fainting. All this was alien to her, as was the man Retford. This was his great arena. He was the victor. She averted her eyes, waiting for the moment when she could slip out without attracting attention. Suddenly, desperately, she needed fresh air. She couldn't endure another blue glance.

Out in the street, she mastered her panic, and now she allowed herself to think he hadn't recognised her at all. Surely a Q.C. could scan a courtroom if he wished. It was all the fault of his blue eyes. No one could be indifferent to that regard. It would be invaluable in cross-examination, a veritable sapphire blaze.

Hours later, the evening papers carried the verdict: Not guilty. In the midst of dressing for a dinner date, Rachael found time to read every word. Cleary, for a young man, looked tired and worn, much as he would if he ever reached old age. There was no photograph of his brilliant defender. One of the prosecuting counsel, looking faintly belligerent. Another of Cleary's wife, a haunted little creature. Cleary's mother and father, hard-working, eminently respectable, their lives shattered in a moment, to be rebuilt again. The verdict had been unanimous. Cleary now had a home to go to, but it seemed he had gone home with his parents. Whether his marriage survived was in the future. In a short time the Cleary case would be forgotten. Other front-page stories would come along to take its place.

Rachael dressed carefully, though it was only the usual foursome; Sally and Dave and Brett and herself. They were going to Lucien's, the superb new restaurant on a high vantage point overlooking the harbour. It would be a first time for her, but Sally had given it a glowing recommendation. Sally was a confirmed party girl and as pretty as a picture. They had been friends since their earliest schooldays, though Sally would not, could not, be serious, but she was altogether easy to be with and very amusing. Rachael, the traditional volatile redhead, took a great many things to heart, not the least of them the loss of her beautiful home and its effect upon the person she loved best in the world, her beautiful, honoured, frail and ageing grandmother.

At last she was dressed. Her shoulder-length hair with its deep natural wave sprang back from her creamy, peach-tinted skin with a life of its own. It was wonderful hair, unquestionably. Gran's hair, as Lady Ross liked to point out. Rachael closely resembled her grandmother. They had the same fine, delicate bone structure that lasted. The same amber-coloured eyes, faintly set at a slant, eyelashes and brows a natural dark brown. Both had the same bearing; in the girl an unassumed, easy elegance, in the woman a certain regality. Only the manner was different. Rachael was her father's child, vivid, vital, loving, over-sensitive. Elizabeth Ross had always been extraordinarily poised and self-contained, even as a young girl, not given to excesses of any kind.

Rachel stared at herself critically, then began hunting around for something to wear around her neck, something to complement a deep V neckline. Her evening dress was very plain, a rich tobacco brown, backless, halter-necked, clinging and narrow as a willow, almost a slip. It was beautifully cut by a master hand but it depended entirely on a beautiful body within it. There! She hadn't worn the gold chain in ages. It was one from Gran's collection, a gleaming single strand with a large, brilliant topaz suspended from it. There were earrings to match, and Rachael had her ears pierced to wear them; circlets of plaited gold set with the glittering gemstones. Gran had worn the set when her portrait was painted. Rachael's eyes matched the stones as well, a luminous gold, though she considered she would never be the extraordinary woman that Gran was.

She glanced at herself indifferently, accustomed to her own reflection, but Allie, their housekeeper and Rachael's childhood nurse, who put her head around the door, whistled appreciatively at the vision.

'Terrific, kid, ravishing, the lot! What I wouldn't do for that figure!'

'Diet?'

'You're kidding! I ask you, what else have I got? Incidentally, your beau's downstairs.'

'Tell him I won't be a minute,' Rachael said, looking high and low for her gold evening purse. It had been there a minute ago.

'He doesn't seem to be suffering,' Allie observed in her dry-as-dust manner, at the same time locating the

35

purse. 'Sally's there as well. Perky as they come. Who's the other one?'

'You know Dave!' Rachael said in surprise.

'I know *Dave*,' Allie drawled, 'but this is sort of tricky. It ain't Dave!'

Rachael turned back, puzzled. 'Then who is it?'

'Like I told you, I've never seen him before.' Allie took a brush to the back of Rachael's hair and flipped up a curl. 'Sally's devouring him like a lover. Brett too. She means well!'

'I'd better check,' Rachael said thoughtfully. 'It was Dave this morning.'

'Times change. Sally's pretty fickle, as I recall. Don't bother to tidy up, I'll do it for you.'

'Will you? You're an angel.'

'What else keeps me here? By the way, what about our prospective buyer?'

'What prospective buyer?' queried Rachael.

'Don't simmer with me, young lady. I paddled you as a child, remember?'

'You never smacked me once.'

'My mistake. According to my information, Mr Retford is coming back tomorrow.'

'You're well informed,' Rachael observed.

'That's right. Your grandmother tells me everything. We understand one another. A very superior gentleman, Mr Retford. Very classy.'

'Not *another* one!'

Allie raised her eyes to the ceiling. 'Don't *you* think so? Admit it, girl, he's magnificent. Naturally I'm interested in keeping the family together, and that includes me.'

36

'We could hardly throw you out at this stage.'

'It'd be difficult! Neither of you would survive without me. I'm the classic retainer. I never give up on the loyalty.'

'I know that, Allie,' Rachael said, smiling. 'Gran does too.'

'Well then! I'm asking you to do something for me.'

Rachael gave a brief nod. 'Anything to make you happy.'

Allie was silent for a moment looking at her charge. Smooth, beautiful young face, vibrant young body, the childhood curls settled into thick springing waves. 'Suggest to Mr Retford,' she began persuasively, 'that if you must sell, you'd just as soon see him get it.'

'I'd sooner see him arrested!' Rachael cried.

'Apparently. But he's the appropriate man. I believe he has an extensive acquaintance with all the top people.'

'Pretty nearly everyone seems to think highly of him,' Rachael said bitterly.

'Exactly. How did your day in court go?'

'You seem to know everything, Allie.'

'It's my job. No doubt at all.'

'It was a considerably sobering experience,' said Rachael. 'Harrowing, I think.'

'What was Mr Retford like? That's important.'

'Brilliant.'

'Brilliant, eh?'

'Absolutely brilliant. Isn't that what you expected to hear?'

'Some character, eh? Listen, your gran likes him.'

'You seem to as well. What a coincidence! I thought him a trifle overwhelming myself.'

'Maybe you don't go for the dominant man,' Allie said. 'Handsome, wouldn't you say?'

'Ah, Allie, what's handsomeness?'

'An advantage. Never had it myself.'

Rachael looked at Allie's dear, plain face. 'You're improving every year. Anyway, you've a heart of gold.'

Allie made a disgusted noise. 'Not the same! All I ever wanted thirty years ago was to look like you. You're my idea of a very provocative, mysterious little lady. Not like your friend Sally. Too obvious—that exuberant kitten act. The subtle touch is better. How come you like this Sally so much? I've never taken to her myself.'

'Sally's fun.'

'I'll grant you that. She's displaying a very lively interest in your young man at the moment. No scruples.'

'Sally's a natural vamp,' Rachael said, quite unconcerned.

'I'll say!'

'Besides, Allie dear, and make a mental note, I don't *have* a young man. Brett's just a friend.'

'A boy, I agree. A simple, uncomplicated lad.'

'Then explain your reluctance to let me past.'

'Sorry, love!' Allie stood aside. 'Run along and enjoy yourself. I can't remember the last time I dined out.'

'You're a better chef than any of them,' smiled Rachael.

'Granted. But for some reason or other, from time

to time, I like sampling a meal not prepared by myself.'

'I know you so well,' Rachael said, laughing. 'All right, let's have lunch the day after tomorrow.'

'Done. I'll make a note of it. You won't be able to back out.'

'I don't want to. My word lasts.'

'Well, you'd better get downstairs and sort out that little drama. I'm pretty curious myself.'

'So am I, now that you've brought it to my notice.' Rachael turned about, inviting Allie's last check. 'Look all right?'

'I expect you'll get another declaration.'

'Brett's pretty slow,' Rachael said, and smiled.

'That pleases me, even if I don't understand it.'

''Night, Allie!'

'Goodnight, my lamb!' Automatically Allie turned back to the bedroom to straighten up. She would never get the child organised!

It took Rachael a very short time to decide she didn't like Craig Coburn, Sally's latest friend. That particular type was Sally's weak point, Rachael considered. Not that he wasn't attractive, compact and blond, well tailored, perhaps a little flashy, a fluent talker, determinedly friendly, the type that looked deeply into a girl's eyes the instant he met her. Rachael didn't like him. He was older, too, than Sally's usual admirers— the early thirties, perhaps.

Brett didn't like him either, if for no other reason than that he hadn't taken his eyes off Rachael from the very first moment. He clearly found her a very desirable young woman. The trouble was, of course, that she *was*, and Brett was making a good show of hiding his mounting agitation. It was part of his training. Even Sally, who had started out the evening in a swinging mood, didn't like it. In fact her pansy brown eyes borrowed a little green from her peppermint dress. Sally liked to vamp all the men and Craig was *her* date. Rachael, though she was lovely, was not altogether easy to know. Sally rarely had to feel on the defensive when they were out on a date, though she had to admit that Rachael was not deliberately trying to captivate Craig. Indeed she was doing her 'young lady of the manor' act in an effort to discourage Craig, but in vain; he continued to stare at this aristocratic young creature. The only thing that kept Sally in her seat was the fact that this sudden passion wasn't mutual. There was too big a contrast between Rachael and Craig—anyone could see that. Rachael needed someone quite different.

'Well, what are we going to eat?' Sally demanded aggressively.

'Nothing. Just nothing,' Brett complained. 'Craig just wants to change places with me.'

Craig gave an easy, practised smile. 'Surely you don't think you're entitled to Rachael's undivided attention?'

'Oh no. Half of it will suffice!'

'Precisely.' Craig gave his languid grin.

'What are we eating?' Sally repeated, looking harried.

'Lobster?' Rachael offered, though she no longer felt like anything at all. If Craig Coburn was trying to upset her he was succeeding. She didn't want or need his languishing hazel glances. Brett, who really was hungry and couldn't fill his gangly six feet, entered into the spirit of the thing and began making any number of delicious suggestions, while Rachael left him to it, leaning her head back against the padded velvet upholstery of the cubicle. It was difficult to restrain her desire to get up and walk out. The events of the day had proved too much for her, robbed her of her usual sparkle. The restaurant was just as she expected, predictably first class, with a stunning new décor and mirrored walls to magnify the size of the room several times over and catch a myriad beautiful reflections, women's faces, lovely dresses and jewellery, bouquets of flowers, soft lights. Judging from the filled cubicles and tables and the heavy sprinkling of well-known personalities it was operating with a considerable degree of success. She seemed to be the only one finding fault with anything. Everyone else appeared to be enjoying themselves.

Brett consulted her briefly regarding the choice of wine, then she retired again, head thrown back, unconsciously showing the lovely line of her throat, feeling inexpressibly melancholy. Her hair glowed with a rich deep fire against the jonquil velvet, and the soft lighting directed a man's glance to the flowerlike perfection of her young skin. Brett, busy with the wine waiter, had no time to be distressed at Craig's very unconventional glances, but they were costing Sally a great deal in the way of self-control. She felt that she could smack his face for him. Craig was very ambitious, but didn't he realise Rachael was no longer an heiress?

'Any more news about the house?' she attacked in the pursuit of the facts.

41

'Such a magnificent home you have, Rachael!' Craig offered. 'Unquestionably the finest home I've been in.'

'Such a heartbreak to lose it!' Sally murmured sympathetically. 'I ache for you, Rachael!'

'Damn it!' Brett exploded with a minimum of manners and a good working knowledge of Sally's methods. 'Why talk about it now? It can't do Rachael any good. She's here to enjoy herself.'

'It doesn't make much difference now,' Rachael shrugged elegantly.

'You mean you have to move out?' Craig demanded, his smooth face a study.

'Well, yes. We simply can't afford to remain.'

'Rachael, baby, you don't have to explain anything to anybody,' Brett maintained—very fiercely for him, because he was essentially a very civilised young man.

'No, you sweet thing!' Sally backed him up. 'The sad fact is, Craig, the death duties on Swans' Reach were enormous,' she added, her work done.

'Have you any plans in mind?' Craig persisted, obviously trying to visualise much the same thing perhaps on a smaller scale.

'No. Not particularly,' Rachael sighed, not wanting to help him out.

'If you don't *mind*!' Brett intervened, 'I can't bear to hurt Rachael with all this talk of losing the house. I know what it means to her, and small wonder! I don't know how she can trust herself not to scream. I'm upset myself for Lady Ross. A wonderful old lady like that! Mother is equally upset. She worked quite a lot on Lady Ross's charities, the splendid functions she used to have in the grounds.'

42

'I wish someone had asked me,' Craig said facetiously. 'I believe you did extremely well in your finals, Rachael?'

'A real whizz kid!' Brett supplied fondly.

'I was a very indifferent student myself,' Sally said crisply, picking up her menu.

'You make up for it in other ways, dear!' Brett said with no appearance of admiration. 'Actually I was fairly victorious myself.'

'Brett's through law,' Rachael explained for Craig's benefit, though in fact he wasn't in the least interested or impressed, not even bothering to shift his gaze.

'Which reminds me,' Sally threw Rachael a speakglance. 'Did you get there this morning?'

'Yes, I did.' Rachael traced a circle on the tablecloth. 'Now I wish I hadn't!'

'What are you talking about?' Brett looked from one to the other.

'Of course, my dear,' Sally patted his arm. 'You don't know. Rachael went along to the Cleary case. In one of my wigs, if you please.'

'You did?' Brett looked amazed—something he did well, for he had an engaging rather ingenuous face.

'She wanted to see Nick Retford of all people, and listen, Rachael honey, you won't believe this, but look who's just walked in. No doubt to celebrate. Say, he really is something!'

'Who?' With no finesse whatever, just like a schoolboy, Brett whirled about in his seat to stare at the entrance. 'Hah! the great man himself. He's got a terrific charisma. Justified too!'

'And the great man is?' Craig asked, very much put

43

out at all this staring not only from their table but elsewhere.

'Nick Retford.' Brett fell back pleasurably to the table. 'Namely the best. You should ask my dad! I've been sent along to observe Nick Retford many a time. He's an inspiration to all of us in the courtroom.'

'A fellow barrister?' Craig asked rather waspishly.

'Unquestionably the best!' Brett maintained, missing the sarcasm. 'Worlds away from Gerald Fox, in my opinion, though he too gets wonderful results. Retford's more human. The way he conducts himself in a courtroom is absolutely masterly.'

'No shortcomings at all?' Rachael asked with a little bitter-sweet smile that had Brett looking at her searchingly.

'You know him?'

'I've met him. *Once!*'

'He must have enjoyed it. He's looking this way. Surely that's Vanessa Maybury?' Sally asked, looking positively intrigued. 'What a super outfit. They look superb together, don't they? She's a bit old. She must be thirty.'

'*Ancient!*' Brett murmured acidly.

'Don't turn around again!' Sally almost shrieked at him, looking embarrassed. 'They're coming this way. I'm talking to Rachael, in any case. She's tall, isn't she, but I suppose it wouldn't matter with him. You've got to introduce us.'

'No,' Rachael said emphatically. 'Mr Retford wouldn't mix with lesser mortals, I should think.'

'I'm not surprised! Not many people would be in the same street!' Brett said in support of his idol.

44

'Hero-worship, Brett, you'll get over it!' Cautiously Rachael lifted her head, her amber eyes in the ray of light a pure, shining gold.

'Good evening, Miss Ross,' Dominic Retford said in his beautiful distinctive voice, faintly inclining his raven-dark head.

I could have been spared that! Rachael thought, respondng formally, though it was a terrible effort, and receiving a very cool appraisal from Vanessa Maybury as they passed on without stopping.

Sally gave a faint snort. 'Snooty thing! I don't even think she's a born blonde. At least she's not going to be alone with him. They're joining a party. Everyone's smiling. The men are jumping respectfully to their feet. God bless them all. Boy, has he got style! More than any man I've seen.'

It struck the final chord in a bad day for Rachael. Her whole nervous system was in a sudden fret. She couldn't remain here with Nick Retford a few feet away. Facing her, too, as she noted with real anxiety. His blue eyes, resting very briefly on her, just had to be his trade mark, so brilliant was their colour, sparkling against the dark background of his skin. Vanessa Maybury was just right for him. A tall, very cool ash-blonde, easily marked in any company as a beautifully groomed woman, expensive, high-class and intelligent. Her clothes were beautiful and her jewellery though sparing was obviously very valuable. Surprisingly, her light grey eyes darted restlessly about until they marked Rachael's table again, then she removed her glance with complete indolence, half turning her long back in its black and gold glittering cardigan over black silk chiffon.

Brett was plainly gawking and Rachael spoke sharply to him, sorry in the next minute because she was very fond of him. Heaven help her if this was to be a standard reaction to Nick Retford—a complete loss of composure. At least she could permit herself the excuse that no one could overlook him.

Craig and Sally were at that moment having a mild argument over Mrs Maybury's assets. 'Don't like the type myself!' Craig observed in his wry-worldly manner. 'A woman's got to look sexy!'

'And she doesn't?' Brett peered myopically.

'Not so much as a man might easily notice. Too rigid. It's impossible to explain. A woman should look vivid, always manage to give the impression she has been or is about to be made love to.'

'Wouldn't that be awfully indiscreet?' Brett demanded.

'I don't like thin lips!' Craig continued, glancing with inordinate approval at Rachael's moulded mouth as though he found it exquisite.

She moved restlessly and he took this to indicate her willingness to dance. There was little else to do but go into his arms, joining the other couples on the small dance floor. The group was very good, as befitted such a place with its extravagant prices. It was a kind of suffering to have his arms around her, his voice in her ear. She felt like objecting violently. Craig was leaning back now, giving her all his attention, taking her favourable response entirely for granted. It seemed to set the pattern for the evening, but at least the food, when it came, was memorable.

'Why don't we come here more often?' said Brett.

'Dance again, Rachael?' Craig reached out a hand and before she could find tactful words to decline, Brett, who was still lingering over a very exotic sweet, answered for her:

'Go ahead!'

Characteristically Craig held her too closely, enjoying the feel of her lovely body. Her topaz eyes gleamed and she broke away abruptly while his hand came up in complete consternation. There was a glimmer of something, anger, in the depths of his hazel eyes.

'I think I've had enough!' she said, breathing a little fast.

'You can't stop here in the middle of the floor.' He went to slide his arm around her waist again, when a charming, faintly cutting voice forestalled him:

'May I, Miss Ross? I've been wanting to speak to you all evening. You don't mind, do you?' Retford's tall arrogance neatly shrivelled the other man's opposition. Craig faded away with a meaningless smile, though inside he was spitting.

Nick Retford turned to her, drawing her into his arms while she willed her limbs not to tremble. 'What a very expressive face you have!'

She looked up at him quickly. 'You, of course, are used to reading faces.'

'Perhaps as well. I don't think your partner would have cared for a kick in the shins.'

'As bad as that?'

'I told you I was watching you. Some fairly violent feeling was animating you.'

She sighed in acknowledgment, but she couldn't relax with him. His blue eyes were disturbing, sweeping her face, and suddenly she *was* trembling, speaking gaily to cover the instinctive reaction of her body. As an antagonist up to his mettle she was a resounding failure. 'Congratulations on winning your case!' she said, and smiled at him as Jacob had suggested.

He looked down at her ironically as though he guessed the motive behind the slow, sweet smile. 'Did you learn anything from your morning in court?'

'So you did see me?'

'Of course. You're somewhat different from the ordinary. A few little tricks here and there make no difference. I actually like red hair.'

He moved beautifully and she continued to respond to the rhythm of his body, not even knowing how not to. 'What did you want to speak to me about?'

'That was timely intervention.'

'A rescue?'

'Something like that. I expect I shall see you tomorrow.'

'I might be there, yes.' She looked up at him, her hair cloudy about her oval face, her creamy skin almost incandescent against the dark, clinging fabric of her dress. Above average height, she still had a good way to look up at him. Some people might think it nothing but an asset to be seen in his company, but she had no intention of joining the charmed circle that hung on his every word. Perhaps he had had a bit too much admiration and adulation. There was a very definite, but controlled sensuality about his face that she hadn't noticed in the court-room. There he had looked dedicated and clever, almost ascetic. Life was full of pain. This man was hurting her and she wanted revenge. His very brilliant eyes were watching her, behind the eyes a logical, trained mind, one step following hard on another. Thank God she wasn't on trial for anything. Her heart lurched with the realisation that he had spoken to her and she had been staring.

'You don't want me to have Swans' Reach, do you, Rachael?'

'No, but I won't embarrass you with my protests.'

'What is your passion apart from protesting?'

'I get very defensive about arrogant men.'

'Really, I thought you enjoyed it.'

'Don't start cross-examining me, Mr Retford. The probing, legal mind and all that!'

'Does it show?'

'It does, along with my protests. I should have stayed home.'

'Come now, you must get some relaxation. As to protests, they, I'm afraid, might prove disastrous. You must take care not to upset your grandmother.'

Colour flared in her high cheekbones, making her look very stormy and dramatic. 'You think I wish to?' she demanded.

'I didn't say that!' he pointed out gently. 'I'm simply pointing out the wisest course.' Another couple, one a novice, almost careered into them, and for an instant she was cradled protectively against him. Instinct made her lean sharply away, angered and confused by the urgency in her, the odd stirring of her

49

blood. He was unrelentingly magnetic, and by some cruel trick of fate, she was being made aware of his very real fascination. For an instant her glance locked with his and she was caught into a splintered fragment of deep familiarity, as if now, right in front of her, she knew exactly the planes and shadows of his face, his eyes and his mouth, the cleft, not centre, but almost on the point of his chin. If she was studying him, he was giving her equal attention and she was no match for him.

'We'll have to start some time, so why not now? Shall we be friends, Rachael?' His grip tightened on her fragile resistance and she realised how strong he was. 'No, don't dismiss the suggestion so lightly.'

'All right!' she shrugged. 'If you want to be, Mr Retford.'

'I have to be, Rachael. I had the feeling your grandmother might like to remain at the Lodge.'

'I'm afraid I can't comment on that.'

'Yes, you can. A lot, after all, depends on you. I saw the appeal in your grandmother's face when you were being such a horrid little girl to me!'

Rachael almost winced, for it was perfectly true. 'I didn't do it to impress you.'

'I hope not. You would need to do so much more than that.'

'You're very good at cutting people down to size.'

'I'm afraid that's likely. It would be much better if you'd tell me now about the Lodge. If your grandmother really wants it, I'd be happy to lease it to her for as long as she likes.'

'You don't own the Swan yet, Mr Retford.'

'You'll never accept it, will you?'

'I'm sorry,' she said stormily, 'do you expect me to?'

'Don't cry.'

'I've absolutely no intention of crying. How ridiculous!'

'Obviously something is making your eyes sparkle. Would you take it any better if it was somebody else?'

She returned his blue scrutiny. 'Right now, I think yes!'

'Why is that?'

'Surely you've heard of such cases?'

'Instant dislike, you mean?'

'No one else dislikes me.'

'I wouldn't dream of suggesting they might. I was referring to your crushing little dislike of myself.'

'I should never have made it so obvious. Sometimes the reckless side of my nature gets the better of me.'

'You'll improve, you know. Anyway, I'm not floored quite so easily.'

'A gift from the gods, your splendid arrogance!' she snapped.

'I'm determined to like you, Rachael. I could have wished you to be different, but I feel if you show a little maturity things will work out. Sometimes painful experiences are all for your own good.'

'As a whole you're a bitter disappointment to me too!'

Unexpectedly he laughed, so that she just wanted to curl up quietly in a corner. 'I expect I sound like a spoiled brat?'

'You ought to do something about it.'

'None of us is perfect, Mr Retford.'

51

He brought his blaze of blue eyes back to her. 'What about the Lodge?' he asked so compassionately that all the fight went out of her. In the reckoning he would always win.

'I don't think my grandmother could bring herself to suggest it to you. She's a woman of great sensibility.'

'You resemble her in other ways,' he said drily.

'Anyway,' she continued, flashing a speaking glance at him, 'I know she would like to stay there. It's just large enough and very comfortable. It's entirely up to you. My grandmother thought perhaps you wouldn't want us on your doorstep.'

'It would be a privilege to see Lady Ross frequently.'

'Thank you. I can see you're prepared to overlook me.'

'That would be difficult, Rachael. Actually I see you with great clarity.'

'I don't much care where I go.'

'You love your home, don't you?' he asked with profound and extraordinary charm.

'I've always had a love affair with the Swan.'

'Except now it's time to start considering mortals. Your companion seemed very taken with you, incidentally.'

'I met him tonight for the first time. He's with my friend Sally.'

'Poor Sally!' He glanced over her head.

'Not poor Sally. It was very nearly because of you I came. I found today very harrowing. Usually Sally is fun. I felt desperate for a little blessed relief from problems. Being forced out of one's beloved home.'

'It's Lady Ross *I* feel for,' he told her. 'You'll be

52

sharing your life with some man in due course. You'll have, very likely, a beautiful home of your own.'

'That's news to me,' Rachael replied firmly.

'No news, Rachael. I daresay you could be married tomorrow if you wished.'

'If I told you I had no intention of marrying?'

'I wouldn't believe you. In fact, I'm surprised at the mature age of what, twenty? you haven't fallen in love.'

'I prefer to arrange my life better!' she said with young arrogance.

'What a pity things don't work out like that. One's whole life can be changed in the course of a few minutes, Rachael.'

'I know that,' she said, and frowned at him. 'I'm not a child.'

He looked closely at her and smiled, a very attractive, speaking, smile. 'Perhaps not in everything, but you're very egotistical, like all born beauties.'

'I am not!'

'No, perhaps it will take a few years more. The beauty, I mean. Please don't attack me.'

'I want to so much!' she said bluntly.

'Doesn't that strike you as odd? I'm sure it's odd.'

She was bristling, left stranded by his cunning tactics, but it was not in her nature to give in. 'There are some things one can never take with composure, and I don't mean all your little digs!'

'The misery of it, Rachael! Don't you really think I know how you feel?'

But she had withdrawn from him, frantic now to make her escape. It was a good opportunity too to get her own back. 'Mrs Maybury is looking this way,' she said, like a small volcano. 'I suppose the next time I see you congratulations will be in order.'

'I'll let you know, Rachael, the exact date of the occasion.'

'You look as if you want me to apologise for something.'

'That would be too big a shock. I'll escort you calmly back to your table. That will show just what good friends we are.'

'At your insistence.'

'Easy, Rachael!' he said as if she was nothing more than a nervous, high-strung small creature of the wilds. His control of her was a bitter pill for Rachael to swallow. He was at her shoulder—tall, very elegant, and she could have rushed to the ends of the earth to get away from him. When Sally saw them coming, she broke into a wonderful smile, her dark eyes filled with admiration.

'Hello there!'

Somehow Rachael got through the introductions, poor old Brett almost overcome with the honour, though blessedly he said nothing out of place. She was almost trembling, torn by contending forces. Nick Retford was, without question, the most striking man she had ever met, his clever, probing eyes holding her, yet he had undertaken so confidently, so callously to ruin her life. There were other properties he could snap up and buy. She turned away from him with a jerk, her amber eyes like golden lightning. Sally, on the other hand, looked as if she might reach out a hand and grasp the arm of his jacket. Even Mrs Maybury, so handsome in her cold way, was craning her long neck. For her soon-to-be-fiancé to spend a few minutes with some chit of a girl was the absolute limit. What an idiot I was, Rachael thought, to have come. She almost stumbled past Craig, who grasped her so tenderly and unnecessarily around her narrow waist. She could have hit him, and all of a sudden she looked up and caught the sardonic laughter in Nick Retford's blue eyes.

'I'll see you tomorrow!' she said, in a mad changeable mood.

Sally glanced at her sharply as if she had revealed some enormously scandalous secret, but Retford only bowed slightly, looking more than ever amused. 'I shall look forward to it, Rachael. Nice to have met you.' Blue eyes flicked around the table, embracing every one of them. No wonder he was famous. Even Craig, his natural enemy a few moments before, looked gratified.

'Pinch me,' Sally said a few minutes later. 'Did I meet the great Nick Retford or didn't I?'

'He did speak to you, yes,' Rachael answered shortly.

'It seems to me, Rachael, you're a dark horse,' Sally retaliated.

'Wait until I tell Dad,' Brett said enthusiastically.

'I didn't think your father was interested in shooting down celebrities?' Rachael said grimly, and closed her eyes.

'You're tired!' Brett whispered in a comforting tone. 'Would you like me to take you home?'

'If I stay here I might start to bawl.'

'What's with you tonight?' Sally asked urgently. 'We can't very well come with you. It's still early.'

'Please stay on!' Rachael said, looking suddenly contrite, the light falling across her face and her sumptuous hair.

'We'll make out!' Sally answered grudgingly. All these past hours Rachael had been acting oddly, and now it seemed she was trying to make a run for it. Perhaps it was due to Craig's depressing, unbelievable behaviour. He had already started upwards, a prey to regret as Rachael gathered her evening purse and the triangular shawl, matching her dress, that she sometimes wore mantilla fashion over her head. The miracle was they didn't have to walk past Nick Retford's table on their way to the door. There was plenty of opportunity for him to study her like a butterfly tomorrow.

Alone with her at last, at least Brett was pleased. Dear Brett, so kind and so near! She couldn't very well have a love affair with Brett; he reminded her too much of the schoolboy he had so recently been. If she must experiment it would be with someone much older. Someone totally different from Brett, though Brett had a special faculty for calming her. *If only!* ... incredibly her mind was running on the most peculiar channels. Could the red wine be making her feverish? As she wouldn't speak herself, Brett had taken, of all things, to giving her Nick Retford's entire legal history. She was forced into listening whether she liked it or not. She could never see him the way Brett did, with awe and admiration. She was made of much sterner stuff. It would be hellish to live in the Lodge with Nick Retford around. She would be for ever running into him.

She wanted to scream. He was taking over her past and leaving her with no future. All the lovely past pattern of her life soon would be gone. But Gran was more important than anyone else in the world. She was too fragile now to shift further. She would live out the rest of her days in constant view of the swans. It was more than Rachael could endure to know Nick Retford had needed no one to suggest the Lodge to him. She must remember he was a very clever man, and her continuing opposition to him would certainly influence her grandmother. There would be, in time, other buyers. In six months perhaps the credit squeeze would ease, but they could not afford to wait. Nick Retford would help them and at once. No doubt Mrs Maybury would be joyously excited with such a future carved out for her. They had, both of them, kicked and trampled on her dreams. Living away from Swans' Reach would be like living in a foreign country, and to have Nick Retford in the Big House seemed a betrayal. She felt consumed with anger and resentment.

Brett was still raving on about his brilliant and honourable record, and Rachael felt like whimpering in self-pity. At least Gran felt at home at the Lodge. It had been built as a private retreat for Margaret Ross who had made the long voyage out from Scotland to join her favourite son, James. James had made of it a most desirable home for his mother's lifetime. Afterwards it had been used very gratefully by relatives and guests who found the comfort and privacy just right. Nick Retford had wasted no time making the suggestion, and all of a sudden her rage against him evaporated. Something they both had to learn was not to upset the ageing Lady Ross. The years of her decline had to be passed without turbulence or personal vendettas. She, Rachael, would have to compose herself always in his presence and that of his so charming fiancée. It would be a close call because she had always been very headstrong and—what? *Egotistical.* There, he had said it. An exceedingly disturbing man. Brett was speaking to her and she turned to him with an effort.

'Goodness, darling, I thought you'd just died!'

'It's just as well I'm not always like this,' sighed Rachael. 'Nick Retford is the one who wants to buy Swans' Reach.'

'Good God!' Brett cried. 'Suddenly I see light.'

'I hope so! That car will be on us in a minute.'

'Poor old kid!' Brett murmured, all sympathy.

The melancholy in her beautiful eyes deepened. 'I had to tell you.'

'Thank you. We've been friends since the third grade.'

'I didn't tell Sally,' she went on.

'I should think not. She's such a gossip.'

'You don't like Sally, do you?'

'She's too easy to make out. I like beautiful, mysterious girls with hot tempers and topaz eyes.'

'Then I'd better change. It's nothing to be proud of, a hot temper.'

'I can prescribe a good medicine. Marry me.'

Rachael didn't even answer him. She looked neither gloomy nor happy. She hadn't, in fact, even heard him. Brett stared at her. Nothing about Rachael escaped him. 'You weren't at all polite with the great man,' he said quietly. 'Not your usual charming self at all!'

'Well, you were so respectful yourself.'

'I have a solid basis for my respect.'

'Suit yourself,' she shrugged.

'Don't be like that, Rachael. I hate to see you so downhearted. I know you can't be cheerful about losing Swans' Reach, but you have nothing to complain about with Nick Retford as a prospective buyer.'

'Excuse me,' Rachael said wearily, 'but I don't want to talk about him any more. Monarch of all he surveys.'

'The funny thing is you seemed to enjoy dancing with him.'

'I did not at all!'

'Now who can make women out? If it wasn't so damned silly I would go further and say you looked passionately interested in him, and he never took his eyes off you either.'

'Why so dramatic?' Rachael sat up straight in the bucket seat of the car. 'What about that ghastly Craig?'

'Sally often makes mistakes,' Brett pointed out coolly. 'Anyway, Coburn's no account. I was talking about Nick Retford.'

'He's coming tomorrow and bringing Mrs Maybury.'

'Goodness, that makes for complications! Women just don't get on with other women.'

'No news. True, I didn't take a fancy to her myself, though she's predictably right for him.'

'Now I didn't think so at all. Not up to his level, for all her superficial gloss.'

Rachael looked at him in surprise. 'What's all this, Brett? It's not like you to be so critical.'

'I, too, had a good long look at Mrs Maybury. She doesn't look a very stimulating woman.'

'Uncle Jacob said she was very witty.'

'Then I suppose she must be. I still wouldn't have

her at my parties looking down her nose at us. She's super-regal.'

'She wasn't delighted to see me, either!' Rachael observed as though the thought had suddenly occurred to her, which indeed it had. Mrs Maybury's pale scrutiny had been quite piercing. She obviously had acquired some modest skill from Nick Retford.

'Wonder where she met him?' mused Brett.

'Oh, they belong to the same set, I suppose.'

'He's no pleasure-seeker!' Brett maintained staunchly.

'All I know is, he wants Swans' Reach and he's going to get it!'

'Simple for a man like that, I suppose. What a pity Mrs Maybury is so close to his heart. I don't fancy her taking your place.'

'I suppose I could always marry him myself!' Rachael said sarcastically.

'I sincerely hope not,' said Brett. 'I'm nearer your age and I'll be making pretty good money soon.'

'Not in Mr Retford's epic proportions. Don't let's talk any more about him, otherwise I'll start to work up a hate again.'

'Argue as you will, kiddo, I don't believe you hate him at all.'

'Meaning I'm not being honest with myself?'

'If you want to put it that way, yes.'

'I can take it, Brett. Besides, Mr Retford is not a man to be bothered by any spoilt young woman's feelings, and that's what he thinks of me. Spoilt rotten.'

'I'm afraid Sir Lewis treated you like a princess.'

Rachael nodded simply. Her grandfather had.

'Perhaps I'm putting that a bit strongly, Rachael.

God knows I think you're marvellous. You've no vanity and tonight you look ravishing. I never thought such a funny colour could look so good on you. All I want to do is make love to you, but we're both so respectable. Besides, Allie would brain me. She's the best security in town.'

'I love Allie. She's a special kind of person. Gran and I would be lost without her. She attends to just about everything.'

'It's as plain as the nose on your face both of you need protection. Your grandfather lived a different kind of life. You know, the old school with a whole lot of rules. One of them was to put his womenfolk on pedestals.'

'I must say I like your frankness. My grandmother is wonderful in every detail.'

'Rachael, wait!' said Brett, holding up a warning finger. 'Your grandmother *is* wonderful. No one in this town will tell you any different. I'm only saying that in some ways she's led a very sheltered life. She came from a well-to-do family and she married into one.'

'She lost her only son,' Rachael exclaimed.

'A tragedy, yes, and I don't mean the way this is sounding. It just occurred to me that your reaction to Nick Retford is characteristically violent. You're used to getting your own way. Small wonder this isn't a happy occasion!'

'One thing I've learned,' Rachael said wryly, 'is when you're down you're down.'

Brett turned a bright red. 'It's your grandmother my heart bleeds for. She's an old lady. You'll be marrying me.'

'Which isn't exactly what I have in mind! You can let me down here!'

They were sweeping between the great wrought-iron gates and Brett groaned audibly. 'Don't let's fight. I really care about you!'

'I'll question that after tonight. It seems to me you've come out very strongly on the side of Nick Retford.'

'Damn it all, Rachael, he's a good man!'

'And you his self-chosen champion.'

For a moment Brett hovered on the brink of anger, then he said quietly, 'I've made this my affair because I love you. One day fairly soon I want to marry you. It's all I've ever wanted. Why do you think I've worked so hard?'

'I think you've been bearing your father in mind.'

'I've been doing it mostly for you—and the parents, of course, but you mean more to me than anybody.'

'Well, you can't come in for supper. You've upset me.'

'That's not very sporting! For the phenomenal price that was a very scant meal. You ate next to nothing yourself.'

'Oh, all right,' Rachael said, relenting. 'I don't want the additional upset of seeing you lose weight!'

'I adore you!' Brett said quite truthfully.

Inside the house, neither of them was astonished to see Allie waiting up. She smiled at Brett, deeply fond of him, but inside her heart she had a very different ambition for Rachael, her own, very special charge. That man must be near enough to perfect. A strong man, strong in the head and the heart and the cheque book. Allie had recently met just such a man. Dimly, because it suited her mood, she began to make plans. Every secret romantic ambition she had cherished so vainly for herself, she channelled in her love to Rachael. Looking across the table at her beautiful, moody, wistful face, she felt a rush of pity for Brett. He was a good boy in every way, but Rachael would need a firm hand. One couldn't live by adoration alone. Allie, in her fantasy, pictured someone very different at Rachael's side. Such speculations were fascinating and nothing was impossible!

CHAPTER THREE

IT was obvious he was alone. He moved away from his
car and began walking purposefully towards the house
as though nothing could keep him from this all-
important appointment. He moved like an athlete, his
lean body disciplined, beautifully co-ordinated. He
looked younger too, dressed more casually, the man
emerging more clearly from the brilliant Q.C. He was
almost beneath the window now; Rachael could see
him clearly. He looked very much the kind of man to
generate excitement. His clothes too had a lot of dash
—a blue and beige check jacket over a fine blue shirt
to pick up his eyes, narrow beige slacks. Gran would
approve. She was extremely critical of what was happening to men's fashions. Nick Retford couldn't have
looked smoother or more sophisticated, and his wealth
was obvious though not obtrusive.

He lifted his dark head as though aware he was being
watched and Rachael moved back swiftly, turning to
speak to her grandmother, who was playing patience.
'Surely you said Mrs Maybury was coming?'

'I thought she was, darling.'

'Well, he's on his own.'

'So much the better! Two women will be quite
enough.'

'Didn't he tell you he was bringing her?' Rachael
persisted.

'Now that you ask me, I don't think he did. Perhaps it was Jacob.'

'Did he actually tell you he was getting married?'

'No, of course not! We didn't indulge in personalities. Maggie told me about Mrs Maybury. She's well up in that kind of thing.'

'Really, Gran!' Rachael couldn't help tutting, 'I'd watch out for second-hand information. Maggie Mac-Adam loves embroidering her stories.'

'Maggie told me,' her grandmother said firmly, 'that Mrs Maybury had been his constant companion for about eight or nine months and that everyone was expecting an announcement.'

'Tell me some more gossip!' said Rachael. 'Gossip. Gossip. How Maggie loves to talk!'

'How long have you been interested in whether he's marrying Mrs Maybury or not?' Lady Ross asked with a quick upward glance.

'Hush, Gran! That's got nothing to do with it.'

'I suppose not,' Lady Ross agreed mildly. 'There now, let's go down. Allie's sure to have let him in.'

Allie met them on the branch of the stairway with the news that was no news. Rachael held back, allowing her grandmother to continue on down the beautiful central section, numb with surprise that Gran was actually smiling and laughing at something Nick had said to her. He was standing directly under the big chandelier with its crystal clusters of grapes, still holding Gran's hand, continuing to talk to her, and Rachael was struck by a sense of anticlimax. She had worked herself up to an emotional scene with Gran, denouncing the usurper and postponing all thought of selling. At the very least Gran didn't have to laugh with him. Soon he would be running the whole show, taking absolutely for granted that Swans' Reach would be his before the deeds were in his hands. Why had Grandfather lived so lavishly? It was so much more of a shock when it was all over.

Exasperated with everyone, Rachael lingered on the stairway, fingering the carved detail of the cedar, cursing Nick Retford for being so good-looking. Gran never shrank from conversation with a handsome, cultivated man. Probably she was asking after the Judge. At this point, Rachael's amber eyes began to glitter. If only she could thrash the whole thing out here and now! It was simply a question of suitability, and Rachael found Nick Retford unsuitable. It was regrettable, but she had thought so from the very instant of meeting him. It was a pity to break up Gran's little interlude. She seemed to be enjoying it, but all females were illogical and Nick Retford was far, far smarter than Gran.

It was bad taste to scowl, so she tried to rearrange her face, but found herself completely incapable of the smiling vivacity other visitors to the house usually encountered. Artlessly Lady Ross turned to her granddaughter, her voice like honey.

'Come on down, darling, and say good morning to Mr Retford.'

Rachael clung to the balustrade, inevitably betraying a little of what she felt. Her golden gaze travelled over his casual perfection. She could feel her heart beating rapidly; she was thrown off balance by the sight of him. His voice reached her easily over the space that divided them, absolutely civil.

'How are you, Rachael?'

She couldn't very well respond as she wanted to, so she merely answered coolly: 'Welcome to Swans' Reach, Mr Retford. You look quite different out of your black robes.'

'And much more comfortable too,' he said lightly, aware of the coolness she was pretending.

'Rachael will be able to show you around the house more completely, Mr Retford,' Lady Ross said graciously. 'Take all the time you want. I'll be in the sun-room. Such a lovely place! The good thing about old age is one doesn't have to make excuses for being idle!'

'You aren't coming too?' Rachael demanded as though her grandmother had better reconsider.

'No, thank you, darling,' Lady Ross smiled tolerantly. 'You know the place as well as I do. I was hoping, Mr Retford, you would stay on for luncheon?'

'I'd like that!' He smiled into Gran's eyes, shocking Rachael further. What kind of game was this he and Gran were playing? The next few hours wouldn't be an easy period for her.

She found it hard to conceal her anger and consternation as Gran moved off to the sun-room with an engaging little wave of her hand. She looked a wonderfully elegant old lady, easy and relaxed instead of trying to pit her frail strength against the invader, Nick Retford. Nothing was going to plan!

He turned his dark head swiftly, pinning Rachael's hostile glance. 'I'd much rather have your grandmother to conduct me,' he told her, trying to smother the laugh in his voice.

'Please try to remember, Mr Retford, you're staying to lunch.'

'Meaning?'

'I can't forgive you everything,' she said strangely.

'I don't think you can forgive me anything. It's perfectly ridiculous, when apart from your unreasonable attitude, I almost like you. I'm not out for your skin, Rachael. The house is on the market.'

'You can live anywhere,' she said at a rush.

He sighed as though the conflict between them was inevitable. 'How would it help you if I don't get the house? Would you jump, for instance, at another offer?'

'You've made the best one!' she pointed out, her expression challenging.

'I understand a real estate developer was prepared to match me?'

'I know nothing about that,' she lied.

'Obviously your grandmother doesn't tell you everything.'

'She does. Of course she does.'

His blue eyes narrowed. 'Let's drop this antagonism business, shall we? At least until after you've shown me over the house.'

'Why are you in a hurry?' She looked at him mockingly.

'Are you?'

'I'm not going to run, Mr Retford. I'm going to stand my ground.'

'You would if you could. I realise that.' He pressed his point swiftly. 'Tell me, Rachael, if I might ask the question. Is it worth it to fight me?'

'I'll risk it!' she said, greatly daring.

There was a superb vibrancy about him; his brilliant eyes studied her as if she were an oddity. 'I think, Rachael,' he said slowly, 'you've been let behave the way you're inclined.'

'Don't you think you're being unkind?' The soft colour suffused her skin.

'I'm being honest. Do you object? You seem to think it can work for you.'

She stood silently, her head slightly averted. No one made her so conscious of her youth and inexperience. 'What do you want me to do?' she asked in some perplexity.

'Well,' he suddenly became businesslike, 'I'm familiar with the ground floor, but I've only glimpsed the basement and the upper floors. Perhaps we can go straight there. Don't look as if you loathe this, Rachael, otherwise you're the most decorative guide I've ever had.'

'Fantasy!' she said acidly.

'No, the truth again. Sometimes, of course, even beauty falls flat!'

'Thank you.' Abruptly she turned and led him up the central stairway. Anger, it seemed, was to be her only salvation, because she felt sick with nerves and something about him made her rush ahead where even a fool would fear to tread. It was all very well to think she could deal with Nick Retford, but having him moving there beside her was proving most difficult. She was passionately attached to her home. Perhaps she was a little proud. But he seemed bent on humiliating her. It wouldn't do to lose her temper, because she was sure he would never lose his.

In the main gallery, well supplied with natural light from a huge glass dome, he paused in front of the full-length portrait of Gran, oil on canvas, in an elaborate gilded frame, the work of a very distinguished artist who had died a few months after the portrait was completed.

'Remarkable how alike yet unalike you are!'

'I could mellow with old age,' she offered briefly.

'I doubt it.'

'Actually I'm supposed to take after my father in temperament. Had he lived, I suppose we might have been in constant friction.'

He turned to look at her, relentless, however charming, his blue gaze long and steady on her face. 'Don't you wish he had?'

'Of course.' She swallowed on another wave of resentment. 'But I couldn't possibly do anything about it, Mr Retford. Both my parents were drowned in a yachting accident.'

'Yes, I know that.'

'And you look as if you're prepared to make allowances for me.'

'Oh, but I am.' He turned away from her to the portrait. 'Surely you wore that same set last night, the necklace and the earrings?'

'You're very observant!' she commented drily.

'I think possibly anyone would notice you, Rachael. You were extremely fortunate to inherit your grandmother's beauty. This is an interesting painting, yet I somehow think it didn't do Lady Ross justice.'

70

'So Jacob says. Grandfather always liked it. He had quite a collection, some of which you see here. Part of my heritage, now to be put up for auction. Every major Australian artist is represented—the early colonial watercolours, the golden age impressionists, Roberts, Streeton, Condor, McCubbin, the Outback studies, Drysdale, Nolan, Boyd. All the younger talent. My grandfather never stopped buying right up until the week he died. He was a compulsive collector, not only of paintings but sculptures and art works of all kinds. We simply couldn't stop him and he used to laugh about it. There are spillovers everywhere, but we don't have to sell the lot, Mr Retford, just the house.'

'Don't go up in flames, Rachael!' he advised mildly, moving to the next painting, another family portrait. 'Your grandfather had impeccable taste. This is a very grand and romantic home, and it's furnished very appropriately. Not everyone, however moneyed, could rise to it. I certainly can't rise to the entire collection, but your grandmother has graciously agreed to let me buy such pieces as I want and several of the paintings. The rest, as you say, will go up for auction. It's a great pity it's a buyer's market.'

'It's affected your bargaining power, hasn't it?' she taunted him.

'No, Rachael, it hasn't!' Evidently he saw no further need to control himself, for his hand shot out and very firmly cupped her chin. 'You must know from your advisers that you're getting a very good price.'

She couldn't turn her head. She could only shake her hair and it curled in a rich strand over his hand.

71

'Why, Mr Retford, have I made you angry?'

His eyes were blue flames, but his voice was cool enough. 'I won't go so far as to admit that, though you're doing your best.'

'I'm not going to apologise.'

He released his grasp abruptly, looking down at her flushed, defiant face. 'Never mind. I'll have to accept the fact that you're a very excitable young creature.'

She brushed past him, going ahead to open the door of the main bedroom. It hadn't been used since her grandfather had died. Gran couldn't even bear to go in. It was too recent, all the tears and the heartbreak. She trembled on the threshold herself. The soft muted colours and the beautiful furnishings, the huge mahogany bed, started to blur before her eyes. Her grandfather had thoroughly spoilt her, loving her from the instant he set eyes on her. If she was outrageous it was his fault. She could even see him at the writing desk. Grief hit her and she walked to the tall windows to look out over the vast green sweep of lawn to the shining reach of the river.

The desire to cry was too strong. Tears stung her eyes and she stared fixedly at a small flotilla of swans. Probably if Nick Retford caught sight of her face he would think her unstable. She wanted to turn around and say something appropriate, but the effort was proving too much for her. Now she knew why Gran hadn't accompanied them upstairs. She didn't want to come into this room. It was too full of Grandfather, dying. The end of their happy life together, the end of the kind of life he had accustomed them to. The intensity of her well-remembered love for him shocked her, hurting her chest, and she put a hand to her heart in an effort to ease the hard knot of pain.

'Rachael?'

Now why did he have such a beautiful voice, capable of entering the very kingdom of the heart? No man called Nick Retford was going to do that. She shifted her hand to the bobbled fringe of the window drapery, continuing to stare down at the parklike grounds. He came to stand beside her, his blue gaze insistent. 'You're a very complex child, Rachael. Was this bedroom your grandfather's?'

'Yes,' she managed to get out. She wanted to lash out at him even though she knew it was unfair.

'The view through this window is beautiful.'

'It's almost the same from the next-door sitting-room,' she answered in a very clipped voice through the tears in her throat. Don't seduce me with your voice, she thought bitterly.

His blue eyes rested thoughtfully on her pale profile, the flame of dark auburn hair that sprang back from her forehead. Tears sparkled on the heavy tips of her eyelashes. 'Rachael, please, you'll make yourself ill!' he said gently. She looked the very picture of trembling nervous energy, too highly strung for her own good, but with such a special luminous beauty and a quick intelligence that it gave her a rare sexual radiance. Again she carried off beautifully a very plain little dress, a mere slip of a thing in a burgundy colour that made the most of her skin and her wonderful colouring. No frills or fuss about Rachael. She didn't need them in any case. If she was lovely, she was also very vulnerable, pulses hammering in her temple and throat. A mixture of a girl. He couldn't decide if he wanted to comfort her or turn her over his knee. It was possible she even understood this, because she turned to him, her topaz eyes shimmering.

'Don't touch me!' she cried in an anguished tone. 'You just buy Swans' Reach!'

'What am I up against?' he said, and drew her against him.

Helplessly she buried herself against the soft blue of his shirt. 'You can't do this. You're my enemy.'

'All right, so I'm your enemy. Look at me! *No?* Why not? You're not one to run away, or so you've been telling me.'

She started to withdraw like a bird fluttering its wings, her amber eyes full of tears. She felt his arms tighten, but she was powerless to block a strange hunger among all her contradictions. She was responding to him compulsively and the situation was getting out of hand.

'I could call for help,' she said raggedly.

'That would upset everyone. Are you sure you want to?'

Some movement, some shadow of an expression across his face was unnerving her. Incredible thoughts and feelings began to move in her head like a passage of music, wild and sweet and disturbing. These last three days had shaken her whole existence, redefining her life in terms of her future. Whatever she needed she knew she couldn't handle it, and the realisation came into her eyes, colouring them a fantastic, glowing, clear gold. Nick Retford wasn't Brett, whom she could wrap around her little finger, a willing slave.

Retford was a natural autocrat, and he was speaking almost curtly.

'Let's get this straight. I'm not your enemy at all.'

'Prove it!' She tilted her head back, for Nick's arms were still linked around her like an unbreakable chain. 'I wish I hadn't come with you.'

'Why not? Aren't we totally incompatible, just as you thought?'

'You don't need to convince me,' she said in answer to his mockery. 'I know my own fatal flaws.'

'What would you list first, inconsistency? All that fiery resentment scattered to the winds.'

'What is this?' she protested very fretfully. 'A paper war. A battle of words only?'

'You haven't stopped talking, Rachael, yet your eyes are telling me something quite different.'

'A judgement on me,' she said scornfully. 'I can always close them.'

'Why do that? I want to check the colour. Last night I could have sworn they were blue, but they're transparent gold.'

'You're slightly crazy,' she said, clinging to the absurd opinion.

'You're no better.'

'But I don't have to be! You're the one with the great talent.'

'I wish you'd remember that, Rachael.'

He was looking at her very steadily, making her look back at him. If she could only ignore the thudding pulses maybe they would quieten. Blue was supposed to be the colour of Heaven, yet his gaze was locking her into a strange limbo, endlessly tempting her. Their whole relationship was brushed with danger. She knew what might happen, yet she stood there as though rooted to the spot, all her brash opposition made to count for nothing against the touch of a hand. The heat of her own body was convincing her of this. It was ravishing, like a game she had never played before.

It was also intolerable. She wasn't going to accept it, such easy dominance. The tension was too much. She clenched her small fist and hit at his chest just at the moment when he bent his dark head purposefully and kissed her mouth. The shock brought chaos to her senses, too big a price to pay for her young arrogance. It seemed to take a long time. It was a new horizon of experiences, spinning her dizzily like a top. She would never have believed it. The whole violence of her opposition was shown to be invalid. The urgency, the touch of his mouth, her intemperate response. The implication transformed her in her own eyes, leaving her weak and exposed, condemned by her own capricious, sensuous, nature.

When Nick finally released her, his hand still lay around her throat, his thumb on the pulsing, agitating beat. It didn't feel foreign, but triumphant, as if it had a perfect right to remain there, gauging her reactions, bewildering as they were, unspeakably excited, unresistant.

'I can't imagine why you did that,' she said a little vaguely. 'It was cruel and it was unnecessary.'

'That sounds like a lament, and so exaggerated. Anyone less suited to being kissed I've yet to find. A woman's words, Rachael, what are they? Her appeal is ageless, but she never says what she means. You wanted me to kiss you. Unconsciously perhaps, but you still wanted it. *Needed* it. A shock makes one see things a whole lot faster.'

'But you don't know me and I don't know you.'

'Well, a lengthy introduction is a bit of a luxury these days. In any case, that's not exactly true. I knew exactly the touch of your mouth. You brought your hand up. What were you going to do with it? Hit me or curl it around my neck? No, you're impulsive, Rachael, and I can't abide by the rules with you.'

'I don't want to remember it!'

'Why, to save your pride? You won't forget it. Neither will I. It was too much to keep up all that crisp young taunting, the sarcastic little greetings. That kiss was a gift. I might have turned you over my knee.'

She tossed her head and her hair fell unrestrained about her flushed face. 'Thank you for your generosity.'

'Nothing at all!' he said tolerantly. 'You're a dream. I almost wish I was your age. Now, that's settled, are you going to show me the rest of the house?'

'Am I to take it I'm forgiven?'

'Rachael ...' He laid his hand on her restrainingly and she lowered the tilt of her chin. The kiss was the worst of all. A slap might only have irritated her. If she was strong, he couldn't touch or hurt her again, yet she wanted him to follow her.

For the rest of the tour, she kept strictly to architectural details, losing her confusion in talk of moulded ceilings, elaborate cornices, architraves and pediments, the cedar joinery, half columns with Corinthian capitals, great chandeliers, very graceful or ornately lavish, huge gilt-framed mirrors, beautifully etched windows, the white Carrara marble fireplaces. He took it all splendidly, though she had the conviction he was laughing at her. In the parklike grounds he calmly observed all the sculptures and the beautiful fountain that sprang up from the centre of an ornamental lily-pond floating the gold and magenta and white nymphaeas.

'I'll hardly have time for all this!' He let his hand sweep broadly down the expanse of lawn.

'Grandfather had three gardeners under contract.'

'And how are you managing?' he asked her, his eyes on her slender figure, the graceful, very cared-for hands.

'Two continue to come from time to time. Mostly as a favour to Gran. I imagine they would be prepared to work for the person who eventually buys the place.'

'That's it, Rachael!' he said mockingly. 'Never let the tension go slack. What a magnificent old home this is!'

'It will have a few ghosts.'

'Are you intending to haunt me?'

His blue eyes travelling over her were like a shock of lightning. Rachael stared at him for a moment in a trance. She could scarcely credit that such very blue eyes could go with black hair and a bronze skin. She jerked her head back distractedly, the sunlight making a ruby cloud round her creamy face. 'God knows I'd like to!' she said shakenly. 'You deserve to suffer.'

'Possibly, but why do you want to make me, particularly?'

'You have that effect on me. Now do you want to see the Lodge?'

'Why not? It's near the main gate, isn't it?'

'Yes. You can scarcely see it through the trees. It was built about 1843, for Captain James' mother. A sort of dower house.'

'And the little pagoda?'

'That's one of Grandfather's extravagances. A folly, a status symbol years ago. To leave all this will be unendurable!'

The misery was in her voice again and he turned to speak to her very directly as though she were indeed a child.

'Look, Rachael, I told you I'm prepared to lease you the Lodge.'

'Now why doesn't that make me happy?' She stared at him, her young face pure and impassioned at once. Abruptly he swung his head away from her.

'It's a beautiful day. You're young and vivid and you've had an excellent education. Such things are enormously rewarding. The rest you'll hurdle. In time these death duties must be abolished, at least between husband and wife. Don't blame me for circumstances outside my control.'

'Anyway, what does it matter if you upset me? We're direct opposites. I must confess I'm dying to know when you're getting married.'

He glanced at her calmly and it was she who looked away. 'You're all mixed up, Rachael. I never said I was.'

'But surely——?'

'Surely what?'

79

'You can't afford not to have a hostess. A life style like the one you're undertaking absolutely demands one. Anyway, there's considerable talk that you're going to marry Mrs Maybury. She's very suitable,' she added, with an expression of eternal good will. 'But of course, if she's only a *friend*?'

His clever face hardened, a frown between his winged black brows. 'If you want to go on with this, Rachael, I might consider marrying *you*!'

'How unreal!'

'I insist I'm taken with you. However, even I can't indulge myself so far. It would be against my moral code to snatch such an infant from the cradle!'

'You had no scruples about kissing the said infant,' she said drily.

'You can interpret that as a lesson. All children need them.'

'I can't afford another one.' She bent and twisted a yellow dandelion from the grass.

'Neither can I,' he said, looking down at her glistening head. 'Did your informants also tell you I have a son?'

'Yes, they did,' she said, straightening and looking up at him quite seriously. 'What's his name and how old is he?'

'His name is Jon and he's nearly eight.'

'He's going to love it here,' she said, and sighed.

'I hope so. It's mostly for him that I'm doing it.'

'You see what I mean?' Rachael challenged him. 'You need a wife.'

'Very well. What about you? You're little more than

a child. You'll be an excellent playmate for Jon. He too is very high-spirited and full of reckless courage.'

'Do you love him?'

'What an extraordinary question!'

Her expression darkened. 'You're not going to send him to boarding school?'

Nick glanced at her curiously. 'Later on, when he's ready to study in earnest. Thirteen or fourteen perhaps.'

'That's all right, then!'

'I can see Jon, at least, has found a champion,' he said drily.

She turned to him, her amber eyes glowing, the breeze skeining her hair about her face. 'I had friends at school who used to tell me they sobbed themselves to sleep.'

'It's all a question of alternatives, Rachael. Most of our country children have to come in to boarding school, at least for their secondary and tertiary education.'

'These girls lived down the road. My grandfather would never have let me out of his sight, and Gran and I have always been like that!' She held up two slender fingers and twined them lovingly.

'You're telling me something important, Rachael. You become deeply involved when you love.'

'Of course. Doesn't everyone?'

He almost groaned. 'Oh, Rachael, Rachael! Love's a word that doesn't seem to mean much any more. I see plenty of hatred in the courts.'

'But love is the core of our lives.'

'So the man said as he strangled his wife.'

Nick's dark head was bent and he looked very serious and remote, his brilliant eyes hooded.

'Is something wrong?' she asked, sounding troubled. 'Is it a case?'

'One I've declined. Some things I don't enjoy.'

'What made you decide to become a barrister?' she asked.

'A family tradition.'

'Oh yes, I remember, the Judge. He was madly in love with Gran.'

He turned to her, an irresistible expression in his sapphire eyes. 'I certainly have no difficulty in believing it. Looks like that would put anyone in a tizzy! Young Vickers, is he a special friend of yours?'

'Brett? We've known one another since the third grade. Nothing passionate, just protective. I'm very fond of him. He's just passed his finals, as a matter of fact. Law.'

'Is Martin Vickers his father?'

'The same one. I suppose I can blame the bar for most of my troubles.'

'You'll have me thinking you're addicted to the profession.'

'I would never trust a barrister, for instance.'

Something in his expression made her nervous. 'You'll have to control your statements, Rachael.'

'It would seem so. Gran will expect us on the dot of one. Shall we look at the Lodge?' She ran away from him over the grass, the wind in her face, cool and scented, accepting his magnetism but willing her body to break free of it.

'There, where's the key?' she said. 'Ah, here it is.'

She plunged her hand into a huge camellia tub, locating the heavy key and brushing the dust off her fingers.

'This is perfect!' He came to join her, standing in the sunlight staring up at the small, two-storey building. The walls were of old brick washed the palest pink, the tiled roof rosy, with white shutters on all the windows. It wasn't grand or impressive like the main house, but it was very charming with an Ionic portico and a protective veranda, lotus capitals on the slender white columns.

Rachael stood there almost nervelessly watching Nick, then he came up the four shallow steps and took the key from her. The beautiful fanlight over the double doors was etched with fruit and flowers, and tall glossy-leaved camellias in pots flanked either side of the entrance.

'A front door should always say welcome!' he said rather suavely, allowing himself a brief glance at her averted profile.

'There's a grape arbour at the back,' she managed. 'It's beautifully cool in summer. I love the beautiful old cypresses, and the flowers always flourish at the front here and the sunny side of the house. I haven't been in for a while. Allie usually attends to things.'

'I hope you're never swept giddily into hard work.'

'I could manage!' she said heatedly.

'What, a brilliant, haughty porcelain figure like you?'

'You can't really believe that. I'm perfectly willing to go to work.'

'Really? What would you like to do?'

'I could always open and shut the front gates for you.'

He glanced about. 'If you will talk like that, Rachael.'

'What it's all boiled down to is that you're taking absolutely for granted that my home will be yours.'

'Surely it's a question of who can afford it. At least I thought so.'

'I must keep reminding myself over and over.'

'Rachael, it's easy to see you resent me, in fact, I expected it, but don't go feeling proud of it.'

'Don't delude yourself—I more than resent you!' she snapped.

'That's perfectly evident. You could hardly have done better when I kissed you.'

'It wasn't intended that way, believe me.'

'I saw nothing wrong in it, Rachael. You're a very desirable child, pure and simple.'

'What sort of an answer is that?' she asked, trying to control her exasperation.

'Deep down, are you really dreading the prospect of living on my doorstep, as you put it?'

'Can't you see I feel like screaming?'

'You want a little mastering, that's all!' he said crisply, his blue eyes very masculine and speculative.

'That's just the difference between the new woman and the old. We don't go in for that sort of thing any more.'

'More's the pity! Women are losing their femininity.'

'You mean we're not confused any more. We won't be restricted.'

'Your size must be a stumbling block. It would be a lot easier for you to get your degree than manage those front gates for me. They're extremely heavy and one of them needs attention. I might be able to fix it for you before I go. If it fell on you it would kill you.'

'Well, if you want to!' Common sense made her retreat. 'Actually we've been keeping them open for just that reason. They came from Italy. Didn't you notice the linked initials J.R.? The ironwork is exquisite, baroque, I think. They were gilded originally, but Grandfather had them painted black, in case someone decided to pinch them.'

'They would have had their work cut out!' Nick turned to flash a smile at her.

'I know, but it made no difference to Grandfather. He was always on the look-out for burglars and prowlers and such like. Even gangs. He thought the world was sinking into degeneracy. At one time he even boobytrapped the grounds. He was a Colonel during the war and he studied guerrilla tactics.'

'Which reminds me of young Jon's definition of a guerrilla. A year or so ago when he heard guerrillas had hijacked a plane he informed me quite seriously that they were "just men dressed up in monkey suits". I think he was trying to reassure me because I was flying to Perth at the time.'

'What else would occur to him?' she asked, and laughed. 'Logical too. Does he take after you?'

'He always seems to do things I used to do. He looks like me, yes.'

'He must be a very handsome little boy.'

He rounded on her, one black eyebrow raised. 'Oh, come now, Rachael, is that a compliment?'

'Funny, I guess it must be. What it really adds up to, however, is that I like children.'

'You don't need to convince me. You have that look about you. Jon is very quick and intelligent and he understands a lot of things. He's had to. His mother died when he was little more than a baby. We've been caring for one another ever since.'

'Has he a nanny?' she asked.

'I have a housekeeper,' he amended, leaning away from her and picking up a small biscuit porcelain figurine. 'Well, well!' he said, and put it down again. 'She's an ex-nursing sister, Rachael, and she's very good. Jon isn't alone much, but unfortunately at one time I had to go away a lot. I hired Stevie then. That's Mrs Stevenson and that's Jon's name for her. Before that he stayed a lot with my wife's people. He didn't care for it, though they were extremely good to him. It was just that he wanted to be with me.'

'Naturally. I suppose he thinks you're the most super being in the world.'

'As I see it, a lot of boys think that of their father.'

'Oh, come now—I mean, after all, there's only one Dominic Retford.'

'What's wrong with me?' He gave her a long level look.

'I doubt if I will tell you.'

'You haven't learned nearly enough, but all in good time. There are some very fine pieces here.' He moved idly about the lovely room, admiring.

'They've been in the Ross family for generations. Margaret Ross brought most of these formal things out from Scotland. Oddly enough they're all French. Gran had the deep sofas put in. The Louis XVI stuff is lovely, but it's not all that comfortable. Blue and white

86

is a very restful colour scheme, don't you think? Gran's choice. It all used to be gold. That mirror over there is very rare, and that's the original glass. The marble-topped commode and the writing desk are eighteenth-century. Margaret Ross brought them out. The place has been re-papered, of course, and the carpeting right through is almost new. Gran had it specially woven to match the draperies. The mirror in the dining-room is ceiling high. Let's go in there. That's the library-sitting-room. Have a quick look if you like.'

Nick did so, then came to join her, looking up at the huge mirror.

'We couldn't find anywhere to put it in the house,' Rachael explained, 'so Gran had it sent down here. Grandfather bought it at an auction. He used to buy first, then leave Gran to worry about where everything would go. He simply couldn't stop even when we'd reached saturation point. I'm certainly glad he didn't bet on horses.'

'Well, it does double the size of the room,' he pointed out.

'Yes, and you can see through to the drawing-room when the doors are opened out.'

They were both reflected in the huge gilt-framed mirror with its knots of roses and fat, winged cupids. Nick lowered his head from his study of them and found Rachael's mirrored eyes. The colour raced under her skin. She couldn't control it and her heart turned in her breast. She stared back at him as if he were a ghost, feathery waves of feeling leaping along her spine. She wanted to speak, to say something witty or in-formative, but suddenly, startlingly, she found she

87

could not. He looked very darkly, vividly handsome, imperious even, his questing blue gaze full of intensity. The very air seemed charged with electricity.

She drew back instinctively, her eyes shimmering in her lovely flushed face. His physical presence was filling her with perplexity. She wanted to run, yet she was reliving the tumultuous shock of his mouth, her mind and her body miles apart. She wouldn't join the ranks of his admirers. This charisma of his was a natural advantage, enhanced by years of training. She was an amateur and her opposition could be judged as artificial, hypocrisy. Never mind about the rest of the house, she wanted to leave now. She couldn't play at this fashionable exchange between a man and a woman and she wasn't even going to try. She didn't know it, but she had made a small sound of protest.

Their reflections broke up. He moved to the doorway. 'Rouse yourself, Rachael,' he said with some mockery. 'We haven't got all day. Now, how many more rooms are there? I'll take your word for it. We'd better not remain here, because there's no guarantee I won't kiss you again.'

'You're just trying to throw me off balance!'

'No, you're very intriguing!' He spoke lightly, his blue gaze in winged satire over her face, but a muscle hardened beside his mouth.

Rachael bent and straightened the centre-piece on the table, her fingers clenching convulsively. She would have liked to throw it at him, but it was a particular favourite of Gran's. She began to speak quickly, rattling rooms off like a real estate agent. 'The library-sitting-room you've seen. There's a sewing-room behind that.

A maid's room, kitchen, downstairs bathroom. The main bedrooms are upstairs, another bathroom and a study. All modern plumbing, of course. The back terrace Gran had glassed in and turned into a shady summer retreat. We've had lots of friends and relations to stay here. It gives them a sense of complete privacy.' She swung up her head to look at him. 'Enough?'

'Very professional. I feel a lot easier in my mind now I've seen it. Some people might count this a small palace.'

'Well, it's not spectacular, but it's very comfortable.'

'You've been brought up in a mansion, Rachael,' he said drily. 'This to a lot of people would be a wonderful way to live. My concern has been mainly for Lady Ross, but this is very charming and quite big enough to be suitable. Shall we go?'

Some of the tension relaxed a bit. She turned to him and smiled. 'I won't quibble with that. I think it's a good idea as well.'

His mouth twisted with amusement. 'Won't you please call me Nick, or Dominic if you prefer?'

'I'll try. What does Mrs Maybury call you?'

'Darling, mostly.'

'I don't think I'll ever rise to that.'

'I'm afraid you don't like me!'

'You'll have to remember that.'

He allowed her to precede him out of the door, then he pulled it to, securing the lock. 'Where do you want the key, back there?' He indicated the big plant pot.

Rachael simply nodded her auburn head, and walked out into the sunshine. The warm breeze carried the scent of the roses, beautifully evocative of every delight she had ever known, the joy of growing up at Swans' Reach. The massive stone gateposts supporting the great wrought-iron gates were smothered in a pink flowering creeper. The estate was at its most beautiful now with the spring flowering. She fought off a quick surge of emotion. This was the Garden of Eden. The variety of trees and shrubs and flowers, as lovely a vista as one could wish for.

Masses and masses of azaleas spilled on to the grass, a collection of Belgian doubles under the trees; the breathtaking beauty of the camellias with many new interesting varieties introduced by Professor Farrell, one of the world's greatest authorities on camellias and a lifelong friend of her grandmother's, some growing in the complete shade and others getting filtered sun through the trees; the sculptures and statuary in the clipped arbours of English holly or guarding the steps to the lower terrace, the vivid green tree ferns and rock orchids that grew near the river, the great pink and silver and flaxen plumes of the pampas grass that matured in late summer. Rachael could weep for the fine halcyon days that were past. Days she would always remember. She was fortunate indeed to have known them at all. All of her friends had envied her. Now that envy would be turned to sympathy.

Nick Retford came alongside her and she gave him a bitter-sweet smile. 'Gran will be waiting. I should tell you she's quite prepared to accept your offer.'

He reached out and caught her hand, holding her still. 'If you try, Rachael, we can be friends. If you won't ...!'

'What will you think of me?'

'I'll think you don't want to be a woman, just a spoilt child.'

'Please, the shoe's on the other foot. You're a tyrant!'

'Exactly. We're trapped!'

No words were necessary after that. They walked back to the house in a fraught silence, Rachael's long slim legs flashing, her high-boned young face clearly unrepentant. The thought of conceding a victory to Nick Retford was too terrible to be borne. From time to time he glanced down at her, his blue eyes brilliant with mockery. It would be a long time before young Rachael would be prepared to accept a man's domination!

CHAPTER FOUR

RACHAEL timed her entrance to the very last moment, coming in through the French doors and taking the seat reserved for her at the very back of the room. The auction was due to start at ten a.m., leaving her precisely three minutes to look completely around the room. Not a seat had been missed. It was almost a crush. She wouldn't have minded, only this was the end of life at Swans' Reach as she had known it. She caught sight of Nick Retford's distinguished head, Mrs Maybury actually smiling, a change from the icy, emotionless blonde goddess, at his side.

Sparks flashed in Rachael's eyes. I haven't the strength, she thought. I can't take it! Not that Gran hadn't warned her, accepting Maggie's kind-hearted invitation to stay over a few days and get away from it all. Why hadn't she been sensible and joined them? This was as bad as a wake, and so crowded. There were undoubtedly many genuine buyers scattered about the room; the dealers, collectors or their agents, the amateur experts; but most of the crowd had come for some exhilarating free entertainment and the opportunity to see over the house and grounds. Three days had been set aside for pre-sale viewing, enough time surely to satisfy the curious, but now everyone had turned out to be in on the excitement of the actual sale even when they knew perfectly well they wouldn't make a bid.

The rich connoisseurs were there in strength. Rachael knew quite a few of them from the old days with her grandfather. There was a goodly sprinkling of her friends' parents. The Ross collection was known to be valuable and extensive. It was no place for the enthusiastic bargain hunter. The real experts lounged in their chairs with faces of utter indifference, little fever waves of buyer's frenzy inside them, conveniently hidden. In the old days this had been the ballroom. Now it provided maximum space for displaying the various collections and containing the crowd. Security men had jostled along with the rest for days, making things more difficult for the auctioneers and their busy staff. Rachael nearly cringed when Pru Maugham, the society journalist, recognised her and waved an uninhibited greeting. She wanted to remain anonymous. A T.V. 'In Town' programme had asked permission to film a segment of the auction for their show and the camera team were in place as well.

Rachael's fingers tightened around her catalogue and she shifted her chair back, ostensibly to catch the breeze. She had dressed to be inconspicuous, but her beautiful flamboyant hair alone would have made that impossible. Many a person dressed up to the nines turned back to stare at her with a: 'Surely that's the Ross girl, and where is her grandmother?' Well, the grandmother had more sense. Less wear and tear on the nervous system, as she explained it to her impulsive granddaughter.

The auctioneer rapped the gavel on his rostrum and

suddenly there was silence except for the high-pitched laugh of some unstoppable lady who behaved exactly the same everywhere. The sale had begun. Rachael found herself unable to take a cool balanced view of anything. That very same morning she had sworn to Gran she would be perfectly all right. In any case she wanted to put in a bid for a very few items in this morning's Oriental collection. She had not mentioned that to her grandmother in case Lady Ross withdrew the pieces from the sale and gave them to her. She could ask no more of her grandmother. Gran had reserved enough for her in the way of several beautiful pieces of furniture, the pick of the porcelain and a few cherished, very valuable paintings. In time they would come to her, but for now she had a little money of her own, a legacy from her dear, sweet, unknown little mother. She had only photographs of her parents, no memories. Had she been an older child she would have perished with them.

From where she was sitting now, she had a clear view of Nick Retford and his companion. They had a perfect right to be there. It was his home already, save for the legalities. Why should that silly blonde woman achieve the impossible? she thought passionately. To replace Gran as mistress of Swans' Reach. If they served coffee later, she would poison it. Gran would be appalled. Hating was a madness, reserved for the thoroughly uncivilised. She would have to stop it. She subsided, vehemently determined to be strong and brave. The house she loved with all her heart, and it didn't seem possible she no longer lived in it. If she gave way to her anguish she would start howling and startle this sophisticated, well-dressed crowd. It was Mrs Maybury who jarred on her so frightfully—that patrician ivory countenance, so cool and impassive. Mrs Maybury was about to be lifted to the skies. Rachael couldn't applaud her. How much wiser to have gone to Maggie's with Gran. This was like tearing one's heart out.

While Rachael sat there warring with herself, various lots had gone swiftly. The bidding had been immediate and brisk, in marked contrast to many an auction Rachael had attended with her grandfather when everyone remained mute waiting to see what Sir Lewis would do. The methods of communication were still the same, the unobtrusive nod, the falling finger, the shake of a page, the more open crisp tone, and occasionally someone like Grandfather who frightened off the opposition on his manner alone. The psychological aspect was important. Bidding was strongly influenced by action and reaction. At least Grandfather's things were being sold to the satisfaction of the auctioneers. Mr Edwards, the head of the firm, had already directed towards her a bracing, encouraging glance.

Rachael jotted down the prices on her catalogue, her passion so forcibly restrained that her pen kept piercing the paper. Gran had said emphatically: 'I can't go and I won't go!' Why hadn't she said the same? It was clear this was exacting too much from her. Grandfather would turn in his grave at some of the prices. How she had loved him, and he had gone and left them. By the end of the day she would be a raving lunatic. This was not a happy occasion, yet from the sudden radiance on Mrs Maybury's face, Rachael guessed that the new owner had just asked him to marry her. At least they wouldn't have all the furniture. That would have been too much of a good thing. The most valuable and rare pieces had a reserve price on them, but Gran had instructed the auctioneers to let most of the things go. They had nowhere to put them in any case.

To her astonished realisation she succeeded in getting the lavender jade vase. The next items were glazed pottery from the T'ang Dynasty, temporarily taking up the attention of the big dealers and collectors. A pair of pottery horses followed the vase. Now she wanted the famille verte vases, the blanc-de-chine seated Bodhisattva and perhaps, if she had any money left, the blue and white covered jar with the dragon chasing the pearl. It was a kind of madness, this collecting, and now it seemed she was into it, with Grandfather sitting not very far away from her regarding her with his fine dark humour-filled eyes.

'I told you so!' Her eyes filled with tears at the thought and she blinked them away fiercely, her glowing head down. Someone from the floor made a witty remark and everyone laughed, but Rachael looked neither left nor right, not even hearing. Later she found out it had been Nick Retford, the legal lion. There was all the time in the world to laugh once she had recovered from the shock of losing her grandfather, then losing her home. She must try now in every way to make Gran feel protected and secure. There would be money enough. They could pay off the government and thank them for ruining them. Or as Nick Retford had been at pains to point out, they still would be living in some style but not on the scale they were used to.

Especially her grandmother, who had enjoyed sixty years of it.

The vases came up in an hour's time. The bidding got out of hand immediately. Rachael had to forgo them. The Bodhisattva should come up shortly before the noon break. An eighteenth-century Kuan Yin, the most beautiful white porcelain ever made. Number 184 seemed to be buying a good deal, she thought, and marked down a price. The Ming jar for that price was a real victory. It had been one of her grandfather's favourites, nearly fifteen inches high. Mrs Maybury, she noticed, had bid for and had marked down to her an octagonal jardinière. Rachael wondered briefly where she might put it. Why limit herself to a jardinière? In a very short time she would be the wife of a rich man. The Judge too was old and ailing, and hadn't he vowed Nick Retford would be his heir?

There was something very noble and sad about forgoing all this. Maybe it would have been better for her character had she come up the hard way. What were possessions anyway? By the time she could work out an answer the Bodhisattva had come up for sale. The family compulsion, only just realised, drove her. She went much higher than she intended, carried away by her desire to have it. Damn it all, didn't it belong to her? This auction was an upsetting, unforeseen element. Significant glances burned in the air at the sight of her lovely, at that moment imperious face. A lot of them weren't in the least kindly but chiding. In fact she was attracting so much attention that all of a sudden she gave it up. She just wanted to fold into a cupboard where she could do a great deal more good than sitting here with every eye and ear on her.

Let someone else have it. In time, she reminded herself hotly, she would own far more valuable pieces, but she had so wanted that piece, bought with her own money. The delicate, detailed modelling of the goddess was exquisite. At the very last moment, Number 184 pounced again. Rachael didn't approve of his hit-and-run tactics. His call sign must have been worked out in advance. At the very least it was heartening to know Mrs Maybury hadn't got it. She had turned her blonde head to stare at Rachael in utter amazement as though denying her the freedom to bid for anything. Rachael had bleakly acknowledged Nick Retford's grave, somehow sympathetic salute. Perhaps he had had a change of heart or was moved to despair by her problems and family predicament. What was most perturbing was that Gran considered him a fine man, a state of affairs Rachael didn't find in the least cheering. He would be a fool to let Mrs Maybury get away. She was without doubt the most beautifully groomed woman in the room, though there were quite a few who usually graced the society pages. She would even make a very good mistress of a home like Swans' Reach. A joyless thought, but there it was.

By the noon break Rachael had a thumping headache. The auction seemed like the ultimate unreality. It couldn't be happening. She was living a bad dream and in the morning it would go up in smoke. It was a good deal harder again to avoid the friends and acquaintances, the name-droppers, who now seemed to swarm around her like soldier ants. Her creamy skin was too pale and her amber eyes had darkened. Here she was with her heart torn and she had to behave congenially, like a clown. This one and that one insisted she sit with them. Sally's mother was there like a gorgeous plump hummingbird, bent on supporting her little girl's dearest friend. It was a moment of horror until she heard a well-known voice at her side.

'How are you, Rachael?' A very blue gaze swept the small gathering, charming them with a quite insincere apology. 'You'll excuse us, won't you? Rachael has promised to share the coffee break with me.'

Mrs Logan, Sally's mother, was about to say something, but she gave up after a moment's hesitation, seeing she couldn't win anyway. It would have been very pleasant indeed to join Nick Retford for coffee, but obviously he wasn't offering to invite her. What could he possibly have in common with Rachael? She was only a child, very pretty certainly, if you liked redheads, but no more pretty than Sally, who had a different, more effervescent quality inherited from herself. Not for a moment was Mrs Logan going to open her eyes to Rachael's extraordinary beauty, unlike Vanessa Maybury, who was regarding the girl with anger as well as frustration. It was inevitable that Nick would wish to shield the girl. He was that type of man, the old school. The ruthless look he assumed from time to time was only a mask. Nick was unique, a very clever and exciting man, but he was also a man who responded to beauty.

Vanessa had worked on her own appearance nearly twenty-four hours a day for the past eight and a half months. She couldn't be detached about the way Nick looked at any other woman. He had his dark head inclined almost protectively towards the Ross girl, who already had too many of the good things in life. So they had lost the house, what of it? What was so mystical about a house? Vanessa's pale grey eyes brooded over the little tableau in front of her. She simply couldn't back away from Nick Retford. She would be thirty-one in December and her own beauty would begin to shrivel. For a very cool-looking woman, Vanessa was moved quickly to anger and aggression. Why, she would be perfect for all this, and not one of her friends disagreed with her. When Nick had told her he was thinking of buying the old place, she was thrilled out of her mind, seeing herself immediately in just such a garden setting. This idiotic Ross girl wasn't going to make her the laughing stock of her circle, for Vanessa, in the way of all women with something to lose, had seized on the curious affinity between Rachael and Nick Retford, for all their supposed differences. They even looked as if they were conspiring against her. It was not to be borne. Vanessa broke away from her own chattering friends, with a simple nod and a wave of her hand, drifting elegantly in the direction of the recalcitrant pair.

Rachael, in turn, was at that very moment declining an invitation to meet Vanessa, whom she was prepared to detest, for all her fashionable and glossy appearance.

'I'm sorry,' she said in answer to Nick's suggestion. 'Don't ask me to meet your future bride.'

'Why ever would you mind?'

'It's silly, I know, but I can't take any of this gracefully. I'd have to be Gran's age.'

'I can't begin to interpret that literally, Rachael.'

'I mean I don't see Mrs Maybury as Gran's successor.'

'That's natural enough. Meet her, you'll adore her.'

'Not in a lifetime.'

'Well, you'll have to!' he said, looking over his shoulder. 'She's coming this way.'

Rachael, of course, had been brought up to maintain her good manners even under attack, but she wasn't in the least blinded by the apparent charm in Vanessa's smile. The pale grey eyes took Rachael apart and put her neatly together again. Nick introduced them and did it well. He was very good at that sort of thing, Rachael conceded, briefly returning Vanessa's smile. Somehow by just being there he was achieving an unjustified impression that this was a friendly group full of mutual goodwill.

Used to dissecting and analysing people, Nick knew at once that Vanessa had formed the more thorough dislike of the two, though she struck just the right note of friendly sympathy for Rachael's personal crisis, losing Swans' Reach, the symbol of the Ross family's wealth and position. She even asked after Lady Ross in a very soft, confidential tone. It couldn't have been bettered, the reassurance and the empathy in the face of suffering, and Rachael was suffering in her way. In time she might adapt herself to the changing scheme of things, but for now she had to get as far away from this auction as possible. Just to confirm his impression she murmured apologetically:

'It was very nice to have met you, Mrs Maybury. I wonder if you would excuse me. I have a headache. I feel I need an aspirin or something.'

101

'Poor dear!' Vanessa said instantly. 'How terrible! I wish I could get you something, but I don't carry aspirin or anything like that.'

'Well, don't take it too seriously,' Rachael said in the pause.

'I'll walk down with you to the Lodge,' Nick offered. 'You'll feel better when you've had something to eat.'

'What about me?' Vanessa smilingly inquired.

'Your friend Ronald is trying to engage your attention now. He'll gladly look after you. I won't be long, Vanessa. Sit back and relax for ten minutes.'

'I suppose I could try, but it's difficult when you're not there, darling.'

Keep that up and you'll lose him altogether, Rachael thought, looking from one to the other. Not that she cared, she just wanted to race right through the door, out of this close atmosphere of amiable chat. Not one of them rightfully belonged there. In no time at all the whole place could go to the devil.

Vanessa's punishing gaze met that of the younger woman. How awful to feel the way you do! it said plainly. But don't blame me, dear. Make a clean break, and don't consider for a moment associating with my soon-to-be-fiancé. That would be the sublime folly.

'No doubt we'll meet again, my dear,' she said, turning at last to rejoin her friends, most of them with a fortifying cup of coffee in their hands.

'I'm afraid Mrs Maybury doesn't like me,' Rachael said simply.

'If you want to put it that way. You don't like her.'

'I like your frankness anyway. I really do have a headache, and you don't have to come with me.'

'It's as plain as the nose on your face you're only just standing up. Why did you come, anyway?'

'There were a few things I wanted.'

Nick took her by the elbow and led her with great concentration through the crowd, most of them looking on with penetrating interest. When they were out in the garden he turned to her again, picking up the conversation. 'Such as?'

'Oh, mostly the Kuan Yin, you know, the blanc-de-chine Bodhisattva.'

'Why didn't you withdraw it from the auction?'

'Gran has given me enough. I wouldn't dream of asking for another thing. This was with my own money. My mother's money really. All I have left of her.'

'Do you still want it?'

'Of course I do, but the bad guy got it. Number 184. He'll have the best collection in town.'

'Surely he's acting according to the rules?'

'I think he might be a crook.'

'How characteristically violent! Actually I couldn't help noticing him. I don't think you'll have any worries on that score.'

'Then I'll abandon my irresponsible opinions!' Rachael said wryly, not liking the feeling of deep depression she was sinking into.

'Hey!' he said, looking down at her.

She turned her face up and suddenly, for no good reason, immediately felt better. 'I know, don't tell me. I look how I feel.'

'Have dinner with me tonight?' Nick invited.

'You're joking!'

'Vanessa's being here with me today doesn't neces-

103

sarily mean I'm getting married tomorrow. In actual fact I didn't invite Vanessa. She had every intention of coming along.'

'I didn't expect such disloyalty. Surely she'll mind?'

'It's all very well for her to *mind*, Rachael, but as it so happens I'm a free agent. Would you have me marry Vanessa to oblige her?'

'On the contrary. I'd very much like to come to dinner.'

'I didn't expect such instant compliance from you. You usually give me a fight.'

'Not today,' she said rather sadly. 'Gran has gone to Maggie MacAdam's for a few days.'

'Very wise. Actually I spoke to her on the telephone this morning.'

'I'm amazed.'

'Really? An ordinary, everyday occurrence. She wanted me to keep an eye on you, though she naturally didn't put it in those very words.'

'Why, that's simply not necessary!' Rachael said indignantly. 'I suppose the invitation to dinner is part of it?'

'No. I really want to take you to dinner, for my own selfish reasons. After all, what have you got to lose, Rachael?' He brought her to a halt for a moment, looking down into her face.

She said nothing, his hands on her shoulders. Finally she pulled away from him. She could not meet those very blue eyes. They were shattering. Still later, she would find them even more so.

Allie fussed over her the minute she saw her, affected

herself by the enormous upheaval in their lives. Also, for a near-stranger, she got on splendidly with Nick Retford, whipping up instant delicious sandwiches and joining him for a third cup of tea. No one could have wished for a more friendly reception. Allie sat there, chatting on as though she had known him for years, something Allie didn't do all that easily, but obviously, Rachael concluded, Allie felt free to invite Nick Retford's opinion and offer her own on a broad sweep of subjects. To put it mildly, Allie had almost celebrated Nick Retford's arrival and just to make the happy occasion complete, he had invited Rachael to dinner.

With Lady Ross in town there was no point in Rachael's sitting about moping. That was no fun and Allie was adamant, stuck with the picture of Rachael pining away because she couldn't eat the sandwiches for lunch. Allie felt like going out herself, but there were too many things to lock up. In the late afternoon she went over to the big house herself to collect Rachael's purchases. When Rachael came downstairs she would show her where she had displayed them. Rachael wasn't so very different from her grandfather after all. No matter how much they had in the way of antiques, there was always room for one more.

When Rachael finally came downstairs, dressed for her evening out, Allie sprang to her feet happily.

'Cheers!' she cried, flashing the bottle of wine she had opened earlier on and had to finish all by herself. 'You look lovely in white.'

'I thought I looked like a ghost.'

'A ghost with red hair?' Allie almost screeched, as

105

prejudiced about Rachael as Mrs Logan was about Sally.

'I was going to ask you if I'd better change it.'

'You'd better be quick, but *no*! Honestly, love, you look something else again.'

'What's that?' asked Rachael.

'Perhaps Mr Retford will explain to you,' Allie said slyly.

'What I can't understand is how you and Gran have almost clutched him to your hearts.'

'Maybe we're trying to get you back to the house by fair means or foul.'

'Oh, Allie, stop fooling!'

'My mother was on the English stage. You didn't know that, did you?'

'You've told us a million times,' smiled Rachael.

'Your grandmother always accepts it without comment. You're always trying to trip me up.'

'I believe you, Allie, but how do you know? You always said you were an orphan.'

'There, what did I tell you? You think I'm only inventing her. By the way, I picked up your things.'

'*Things?* I only bought one—the jade vase.'

'They had two items put aside for Miss Ross,' Allie told her.

'*Two?*'

'This is getting tiresome.'

Rachael turned about. 'Tiresome? Alarming, more like it. Could I have scratched my nose and had something knocked down to me I actually didn't want? It's happened before. Remember when Grandfather came home with the Lord John Russell. He never meant to buy him.'

'Well, the vase is here. I think you'll like where I put it. However, I can shift it if you don't!'

'I don't know what you're talking about, Allie,' said Rachael. 'Where's the other?'

'Come and see. What's the matter with you, for heaven's sake?'

'You're not talking my language. I only bought the vase, I'm telling you, and it does look nice there.'

'Well, here's the surprise packet!' Allie led the way into the library-sitting-room and switched on the light, then she walked across the room and turned on the table lamp on a small, elaborately carved wood desk. The light spilled in a golden pool over the porcelain Kuan Yin, a small work of art against the gleaming Chinese screen with its peacocks parading in a garden of flowers, and the ceiling-high alcoves of leather-bound books, rich red, black or brown with gold tooling.

'I don't believe it!' Rachael said faintly.

'Go back and tell that to Mr Edwards. He gave them to me, and he doesn't seem the man to make mistakes.'

'I can't imagine how this happened!'

'Oh?' Allie's round face quivered suspiciously. 'You must have had a very interesting morning. Any admirers you don't know about?'

Soft bell tones pealed through the house and Allie came briskly to attention, marching out of the room as though she couldn't embarrass Nick Retford another moment by leaving him out in the night air. They were standing in front of the open doorway when Rachael went through to the foyer. Allie was pink with pleasure at the unexpected gift of a hard-to-come-by recording she had only briefly mentioned at lunch. Nick Retford swung around, his blue eyes appraising the magical bloom of youth, both innocent and seductive.

'You look very beautiful, Rachael, like someone out of a painting. Turn of the century. Just a little unfamiliar.'

'I'm exactly the same,' she assured him.

He continued to look at her and it seemed to her no man had ever looked at her in that way before, eyes touching on the sudden flare of colour in her cheeks, her upswept hair with loose tendrils, the white silk georgette dress with a huge ruffled hand-made peony on one narrow shoulder strap, Gran's lovely old Victorian choker of pearls and dark purple amethysts linked with soft gold. She felt dangerously out of her depth. This was serious. He wasn't a boy but a brilliant, mature man, and he had been married, before Mrs Maybury and others, as Maggie had hastened to mention. His glance troubled her. There would be no peace with Nick Retford. He had too much insight and he could make her miserable.

Allie nodded vigorously at his remark about the painting. That's exactly what Rachael looked like. Something by Sargent, perhaps, a beautiful Edwardian girl. 'It seems we've got this little problem,' Allie began, looking up at Retford confidingly.

'It's all right, Allie,' Rachael suddenly came to life. 'I've disposed of it!' She looked straight into Nick Retford's blue eyes. 'Number 184?'

'I thought you'd never ask,' he drawled.

'Shall we go?'

'Only mention the word.'

Allie looked from one to the other as if they were characters on the stage. 'It's depressing,' she complained, 'but I don't know what either of you are talking about.' She turned around and collected Rachael's gold evening purse, putting it into her hand, implying that Rachael would forget it if she didn't.

Rachael bent and kissed her. 'Don't fret. I'll tell you later on.'

Allie's homely beam was very nearly shy. 'Thank you once again for the recording. I'll put it on now.'

'A pleasure!' Nick bowed slightly, very easy and elegant.

'Shall I wait up?'

'What?' Rachael looked back in blank surprise.

'It was only a suggestion. Let it pass.'

They walked out into the cool scented air with Allie etched in the doorway, waving.

'I suppose she does normally?' Nick asked, as they walked to his car.

'Oddly enough, no. I suppose she knows you're dangerous.'

'In what way?'

'Every way. My well-being is very important to Allie. She was my nurse.'

'And she raised you to your present impeccable standard.'

'Are you laughing at me?'

'Why, Rachael!' He put her into the car, then moved around to the other door and slid in behind the wheel, very tall and sure of himself. It was suddenly like being confined in a lift, and Rachael caught her breath.

'Well, it wouldn't be the first time.'

The car purred to life and he swung it about, heading for the great wrought-iron gates which now, mercifully, hung secure.

'What a beautiful car,' she said, leaning her head against the pigskin upholstery. 'It must have been very expensive.'

'I hadn't thought of that,' he said mildly. 'Its performance is just several notches higher than its competitors'. I haven't the time for breakdowns and mechanical faults and such like.'

'Fine,' she smiled. 'If I could afford one I'd get the same.'

'Your grandfather had a Hispano Suiza,' he pointed out gently.

'Heavens! he bought it in the '20s, and he was still using it until last year. Then he couldn't get his licence renewed, for which we were all grateful. He always drove it as if it were a horse.'

He laughed, such an attractive sound. Rachael looked out the window at the speeding miles, the sickle moon and the windy stars. 'I can't accept the Kuan Yin, you know.'

'Why ever not?' He glanced at her profile. 'Would it damage your reputation?'

'Among other things!'

'Don't be ridiculous, Rachael. You wanted it badly, that was plain to tell. I want you to have it. I have no use for it myself.'

'Then why did you bid for it?'

110

'Perhaps you turn all men into slaves.'

'I'm sorry I asked,' she said crossly.

'Well, let it rest now. The Kuan Yin is yours.'

'Then you're not altogether heartless.'

'I'm altogether in earnest. We're going to enjoy ourselves. No contrary little heiress routine.'

'Not any more.'

'I haven't seen any trace of a struggle.' His glance brushed her beautiful model dress, the lustrous gleaming choker.

'That's Gran's,' she said, and touched it. 'You're not sure if you approve of me, are you?'

'No.'

'That sounded as if it came from the very depths of your very masculine nature. Would you have me scrubbing floors?'

'Well, not in that dress.'

'I just thought I'd bring the matter up. Most men would like to put us on our knees.'

'What?' He considered her profile and smiled. 'The outraged feminist?'

'Why not?'

'From such a female woman.'

'I'm not violently Women's Lib, if that's what you mean, but I'm certainly not going to live out my life in a man's shadow.'

'Jung. Didn't he say that?'

'I don't know. I just read a lot.'

'Most women accept it,' he said, expertly passing the car in front of them, an erratic learner-driver.

'They've had to in the past,' said Rachael. 'This generation won't.'

'So I see from the divorce rate!'

'The logical mind again!'

'What is it you want, Rachael?' Nick asked.

'I just want to be *me*. To be allowed the full expression of my own personality.'

'Well, it's an intoxicating idea. What happens when you marry and have children? A mother's role must be the most completely unselfish one there is—day in, day out caring, constant demands from her family. It's a prison of a kind, but love imposes it. In the course of a lifetime there couldn't be any greater happiness than a rewarding home life, surely? Seeing one's children grow. They don't have to be brilliant. It's character that counts, high principles. I see so much tragedy and violence among our young people and nine times out of ten they're the products of a very unhappy home environment, from every social stratum. The rich man's child can be just as badly off as your battler.'

'Yes, I know.' An immediate instance came to mind, in this case drugs, a promising law student, with plenty of money and mostly absentee parents. She sighed, a very real distressed little sigh, and immediately he changed the subject.

'Where would you like to go?'

'Oh, somewhere very quiet.'

'Fashionable or broken down?'

'You don't look like an habitué of broken-down restaurants,' she said drily.

'Well then, Adriano's. I've booked there.'

'Perfect!' she said, her eyes full of a soft golden light.

She turned her head sideways along the back of the seat. 'You have the most interesting face I've ever seen.'

'Oh? I thought I was only dreaming you.'

'So rarely we're in accord.'

Nick reached out a hand and lightly brushed her cheek. 'Let's stay that way.'

He sounded mocking and indulgent at once and Rachael couldn't deny the sparkling jet of pleasure and excitement that stayed with her for the rest of the night. She had no sense of conflict or inconsistency, just the marvellous, absolutely essential feeling of knowing herself a woman, not just a young face and a slender body. The real thing.

CHAPTER FIVE

To Jon, the new house was so wonderful, the cellar so scary, the grounds, just before dusk, so secret and mysterious, he had to share his elation with someone. This was his greatest adventure since his infancy. With just a week more left of school, he couldn't wait to have the whole parkland and the big house to himself. Of course Stevie was there to look after him and quell his vivid imagination, but his father, who was the most wonderful father one could ever hope for, had to be away for a few weeks on an important case. At least Rachael was left. She knew exactly what kids liked to do and she had given him the most marvellous Chinese kite with dozens of ribbons on the tail.

Rachael, he knew, had spent her own childhood at Swans' Reach, fishing the river and climbing the great shade trees and investigating the clammy, dimly-lit cellar with its glinting bottle bins and the old hand grape press, the vats and the hogsheads and the hooks on the ceiling for the great sides of bacon and the hams they had in the old days long before they had the big freezer in the kitchen. A convict could very well have been interred in those massive stone walls. Probably convict labour had been used to build the house. Why, a convict had even carved the red cedar stairway that glowed so richly and felt so good to the hand. Rachael had told him that. How later the convict was granted a pardon and made a killing on the goldfields, setting himself up as a pastoralist only to be killed a year later by a bushranger. It wasn't as if he had done anything very bad in the first place, only stolen some food for his starving mother and sisters. Jon, who had never gone hungry in his life, understood this perfectly.

Rachael told him lots of stories about the early days of the colony. She was better than a storybook and she knew every nook and cranny of the house and the secret drawer in the writing desk. Rachael and Jon had become very friendly almost at once. The friendship was noted and approved of by his father. Rachael was the person Jon most cared for, next to his father. Of course he could never tell anyone that. He was very loyal to Stevie, who looked after him so well, but she simply wasn't Rachael, who was going to teach him to ride a horse and speak to his father about getting a pony. Rachael had had a pony at his age. So for Jon, each day was shining and full of excitements. If he skinned his knees a lot and Stevie scolded him, Rachael was always there to support him.

Nothing could have been nicer than to have her living near their house. He was welcome at the Lodge as well. Lady Ross, with her pink and white skin, and her piled-up white hair and her immaculate, perfumed dresses, he went a little in awe of. Not that she wasn't always very nice to him, but she was a Person and had to be treated as such.

The other lady, Allie, was quite different—kind of funny, but nice, trying to be friends. For the first time in his life Jon felt truly sheltered. Settled. When his mother had died (he couldn't remember) his father had sold their home and moved to a town house. Now he had bought Swans' Reach for Jon. It was the place to do the most marvellous things; to sing and to shout, to lie on the grass and look up at the sky, or climb to the highest fork of the magnificent old gum. If he got a good end-of-term report, his father had promised to buy him a fishing rod. Well, the fishing rod was his. He was the smartest kid in the class. Mr Tennant told him he was certain to be promoted, but he wouldn't commit himself further even when Jon told him the story of the fishing rod. Still, he was certain he would get it. If it was possible, he felt closer to his father here than ever before. Sometimes he even felt like bursting with happiness. His father would be home in three days. This afternoon, after school, he would go down to the Lodge and give Rachael the latest bulletin. She was always so interested.

Perhaps Allie would have some of that chocolate cake of hers with the hazelnuts on the top. She knew he loved it. Lady Ross would ask him so sweetly and seriously how he was progressing at school and listen very intently for his answer. He would be able to tell her his work was 'highly satisfactory'. He couldn't tell her that he was the fastest runner and the best at cricket; that would sound too much like boasting. Everyone liked him at the Lodge.

When the telephone rang, Rachael went to answer it, leaving Jon wide-eyed with growing wonder at some story of Allie's girlhood. Even the chocolate cake was momentarily abandoned while Jon waited, apparently desperate to hear more. Allie found it very gratifying and consequently dragged out the suspense, one hand resting on Jon's shoulder.

It was almost like encountering a spear, the voice at the other end of the line was so piercing.

'Rachael?'

Rachael held the phone away from her sensitive ear. 'How are you, Maggie?'

'Fine, thank you, dear! I won't bother dear old Lib again, but just tell her I'm *not* having that little ceremony back at the house after the ballet.'

'I'll do that, Maggie. Gran's asleep now, gathering her strength for the big evening.'

'I'm very glad. I can't sleep in the afternoons myself. She does so love the ballet. The little Aldous is exquisite. Surely that's a child's laughter I hear?'

'Young Jon. He's having afternoon tea in the kitchen with Allie.'

'Really? What kind of a story is she telling him? They're making a lot of noise.'

'A suitable one, Maggie. Fit for the ears of young children.'

'Nice little boy?'

'The very nicest. Bursting with life but with beautiful manners.'

'And soon to have a new mummy, I hear.'

Rachael almost recoiled, something inside her shattering irreparably. 'I'm not very bright, Maggie, are you talking about Mrs Maybury?'

'Nick Retford's in Adelaide, isn't he?'

'I believe so.'

'So's Mrs Maybury. A friend of mine saw them together. Next thing it will be wedding bells. You could even be invited.'

'Is your friend very reliable?' Rachael asked rather baldly.

Maggie sounded shocked. 'My dearest child, I wouldn't admit this to anyone else, but she fills me with envy. She knows *everything*!'

'Perhaps you should consider joining forces.'

'What does that mean?' Maggie asked, sounding bewildered.

'Nothing, Maggie.'

'Ah well, it would be very pleasant indeed to have a man like that chasing one.' Maggie paused for the answering laugh to her comment, but none was forthcoming. 'Listen, dear,' she said very kindly, for she *was* kind, 'why don't you come with us this evening? A couple of oldies, I know, but never dull. No, on second thoughts perhaps you'd better not. They won't let you in. The theatre's booked out. Still, I could mastermind something. The MacAdam name should count for something. Eric would have won the Nobel prize had he lived.'

'It's all right, Maggie, I'm happy at home,' Rachael assured her.

'Extraordinary! I would never have stayed home at your age.'

'I can believe it! No offence meant, Maggie.'

'None taken, darling. I know I'm wonderful. People have said to me all my life: "You're marvellous!" Why, I've more life in me at seventy-eight than most women half my age.'

'Agreed. It must be bubbles in the blood or something.'

'If only I were forty years younger, I'd give that Vanessa Maybury a run for her money,' Maggie mused. 'Never taken to her myself. She's very handsome, I know, but she looks all sealed off in Cellophane.'

'On the other hand, she got to Adelaide,' Rachael pointed out.

'Do you blame her?'

'I'm happy to say, no.'

'You don't *sound* happy, darling. Settling down all right?'

'Pretty well, Maggie, considering. I don't know about Gran. She never complains about anything.'

'Now Lib I love!' Maggie cried thrillingly. 'She's a marvel! We're almost like sisters. When we were young we were the prettiest girls in this town. Talk about bombshells! Incidentally, how do you like my new bob? Isn't a fringe silly at my age?'

'On you it's just right!'

'Thank you, darling. How's that boy-friend of yours going?'

'Which one?' asked Rachael.

'Naughty! The Vickers boy.'

'We're really just good friends.'

'Now that takes me by surprise. His mother thinks you'll be getting married in a year or so.'

'A normal mother's reaction.'

'Well, dearest, I have to bathe. Tell Lib about seven-fifteen this evening. That will give us plenty of time to park.'

119

'But, Maggie,' Rachael said, looking more than ever harried, 'are you driving yourself?'

'Of course, dear. Don't infuriate me. I've an excellent record. 'Bye, now!'

'But——' began Rachael, too late, for Maggie had gone. Not that a protest would have done any good, and Gran just laughed at Rachael's lack of trust in Maggie's driving ability when there was no actual proof to the contrary.

So what do I do now? she thought. Maggie's news had made her feel quite peculiar, drained of all sense of expectancy or pleasure. But why? After all, they had all expected it sooner or later. Nick Retford was to marry Vanessa Maybury, a woman near his own age and very suitable from every standpoint. One would expect it, so why had she received the news as a catastrophe? Some deep disturbance was within her, and no amount of reasoning was going to lessen the pain. A few minutes ago, pouring coffee for herself and Allie and a glass of lemonade for Jon, she had known real pleasure, a sense that everything was getting easier. Now the constriction round her heart was threatening to make her faint. She walked back into the kitchen and Allie looked up expectantly, her pleasant expression changing to a worried frown.

'You look very pale, Rachael. Is anything wrong?'

'Perhaps I'm hungry!' she said, thinking she would never be able to manage a bite again.

Allie immediately sliced off a section of chocolate cake. 'Who was it?' she asked, closely observing Rachael's face.

'Only Maggie. Another message for Gran. Honestly,

whenever they go out, it takes at least four phone calls. Thanks, Allie.' Absentmindedly Rachael took the laden plate from Allie. 'They're not going back to Maggie's place after the theatre.'

'And a jolly good thing!' Allie said heartily. 'I never thought much of the idea in the first place.'

'Are you going too, Rachael?' Jon asked, looking up at her with familiar radiant blue eyes, his father's exactly.

'No, I'm going to have my party here.'

'I wish I could come,' he said wistfully.

Rachael was surprised to find her hands trembling. She put a piece of cake in her mouth and found it tasted like dust. 'I'm fooling, darling,' she tried to speak lightly. 'I'm just going to have a quiet evening at home. When I do have a party, I'll invite you. It would have to be in the daytime. It's my birthday next month.'

'How old will you be?'

'Twenty-one,' she said, ruffling his coal-black curls.

'Gosh! I'll tell Dad. We'll have to be thinking about a present.'

'Now, Jon, I refuse to let you pass on that report. It's just between the two of us.'

'And how's that?' Allie inquired satirically. 'People usually celebrate, not go into hiding.'

'Oh well, I do have some pocket money,' said Jon, anxiously lost in thought.

'Which you will keep! I wouldn't think of asking you if you're going to worry about buying me a present.'

'What else did Maggie say?' Allie persisted, her glance very keen and inquisitive. Before the phone call, Rachael had been her lively and very delightful self, laughing and joking with Jon, now she looked almost grief-stricken. 'Well?'

'Nothing much, Allie,' Rachael parried. 'Maggie's driving.'

Abruptly Allie pushed the cake plate away. 'One thing about Maggie, she's never dull. I was counting on someone else driving them.'

'Well, we'd better hold our peace with Gran,' Rachael said dispiritedly. 'She doesn't like to be fussed over and she's very forbearing with Maggie's driving ability. Strangely enough, Maggie's never had any trouble.'

'No, it's her long-suffering passengers that have that!'

Jon looked from one to the other, distressed by the abrupt change of mood. Rachael's lovely laughing face had lost every scrap of colour, while Allie's had little angry patches of red on her round apple cheeks. 'Dad's coming home in three days!' he announced, seeking to bolster the atmosphere.

'So that's why you're so excited?' Allie turned back to smile at him. 'Another piece of cake?'

'Oh yes, please, Allie. It's delicious. I love all those crushed nuts over the side. I've been giddy with hunger all day.'

'Now why is that?' Allie demanded. 'Mrs Stevenson looks very conscientious to me.'

'Oh, I swopped my lunch for a pencil case.'

'I wouldn't advise too much of that, young man,' Allie said, chiding but kindly. 'A growing boy needs to eat his lunch.'

'It was just this particular pencil case, Allie. It came from Rotorua. Higgy thought it a fair swop.'

'Who's Higgy, might I ask?'

'He's my best friend—Philip Higgenson. We all call him Higgy.'

'How interesting. He sounds like an individual. I bet he's got freckles.'

'Yes, he's all brown with them. I'm going to invite him out one week-end.'

'Then we'll meet him?'

'Oh yes!' Jon smiled his thanks at Allie, all the while asking himself what had happened to Rachael. She was gazing into the depths of her coffee cup as if it were a crystal ball and the picture gloomy. 'Are you worried about something, Rachael?' he asked all of a sudden.

'Yes, Rachael, are you worried about something?' Allie chimed in.

'As a matter of fact, I am,' said Rachael, belatedly raising her head. 'But I can't think why. One of those unreasonable things! Now, young Jon, shall we go out and feed the swans?'

'You don't have to if you don't want to, Rachael,' he said kindly.

'But I want to!' she jumped up from the table. 'I've been looking forward to your company all day.'

'Oh, beaut!' It was all Jon could do not to spring about the kitchen, in the mood now for any amount of physical effort, an energetic active child, basking in the easy friendship that was offered to him.

'Let's go seek the sun!' Rachael said, holding out her hand.

'I'll speak to you later, young lady,' Allie firmly

maintained, anxious to clear up the matter of Rachael's sudden pallor.

Outside in the fragrant sunshine, Jon turned up his high-spirited face. 'Do you suppose Dad would get me a dog?'

'I don't see why not,' Rachael reassured him. 'We had a beautiful dog, Glory, a collie, sable and white like Lassie. She was fourteen when she died, and I cried for a long time. My grandfather bought her for my fifth birthday, so you can imagine how I loved her. She had a pedigree this long, though I never did show her.'

Jon considered, his blue eyes narrowed against the silver glitter of the river. 'I think I'd like a collie, too.'

'What about a golden Labrador?' Rachael suggested, still missing her lovely Glory. 'They love the water. Or an English setter. They're very intelligent and friendly.'

'Or a bulldog or a boxer? They could guard the gate.'

'Or maybe a silly, aristocratic Afghan. An Afghan would love bounding about this place, and you wouldn't have to worry about the traffic. Afghans have no road sense at all, but they're a beautiful breed.'

'Let's ask Dad!' said Jon, scarcely able to contain his excitement. 'He asked about you in his letter.'

'Really? What did he say?'

'Oh, the usual things. How were you and what we were doing and a bit about the kite, and he ended off saying, remember me to the rose at the front gate.'

'And how did you know he meant me?'

'Well, actually, Rachael,' Jon explained seriously, 'I

was the one that thought of that. You've got rose-coloured hair.'

Rachael expelled a long breath, laughing. 'You're going to be very popular when you grow up!'

Jon looked up into her face, relieved to see the dazzling topaz glance was smiling once more. 'Do you want to see what I learned at gym today?'

She nodded her head, humouring him. 'Go right ahead, but *please*, don't break any bones.'

'I'll show you,' Jon said confidently, at this point beginning to tumble head over heels down the lawn. After a while, Rachael felt she had to tell him to stop.

'Jon!'

He bounded up, breathless, scarlet in the face, but extremely happy. 'Yes?' he asked.

'Don't tire yourself out.'

'Tumbling doesn't make any difference to me. Some of the kids nearly kill themselves trying to get over the horse, and to tell you the truth, it's no harder than tumbling.'

'I can see you're a natural. And how is your father?' she asked guardedly.

'Oh well, Dad's never sick. He hasn't got the time. I can't wait until he gets home!' Jon stared up into her face as though she too was certain to share his sentiments. It was extremely odd, but she did, her amber eyes flashing. How perverse human nature was! There was a time when she had thought she hated him; now this startling, wounding change of heart.

'When I grow up, I'm going to have a splendid career just like Dad!' Jon was announcing.

'As it happens I believe you,' smiled Rachael.

'Sure?'

'Yes.'

Jon blushed and almost immediately began to somer-sault again, overcome by this moment of mutual affec-tion. He was the luckiest boy in the world. The sum-mer holidays were coming up and he had never felt in such harmony with his world and the people in it. The wind was singing its beautiful shivery song through the leaves, each one of them glittering in the pellucid bril-liance of the late afternoon sunlight. Swans' Reach had a special magic. It had settled his mind, overtaking him with a powerful sense of belonging.

'I *love* this place, Rachael!' he said, coming to a drastic halt and running back to join her. 'I feel as if I've been here for ever. It's not quite real.'

'A dream,' she said rather sadly, smiling down at him. 'I'm glad you're happy here, Jon. It makes it all worth while. Swans' Reach possesses a special magic for the chosen few. Look, all the birds are gathering on the water. They feed on the seeding of the reeds.'

'Aren't the swans graceful? They're like yachts. It's amazing how awkward they are out of the water.'

'We've each of us a special role to play,' Rachael ex-plained. 'For the swans, it's best for them to stay on the water. The land really isn't their territory. It's their job to look beautiful and immortal.'

'Mystical, is that the word?'

She smiled and they walked quietly together, ap-proaching the birds. For all her efforts not to upset a small boy, Rachael felt a deep restraint upon her as though the idea of Nick's marrying Vanessa Maybury was a life-or-death decision, all her own little inexplicable yearnings crumpling like so much tissue paper. Her depression was deepening irresistibly. She would ring Brett, she told herself fiercely, running a hand over her wind-tossed hair, wishing and wishing again she had never laid eyes on Nick Retford. She had known from the very first moment that he would change her life enormously.

Jon broke the little silence. 'Why, Rachael, you look as if you're going to cry!'

His perception didn't startle her—she had become used to it in his father. She blinked rapidly, anxious not to bewilder him. 'It's the swans,' she said, her lovely mouth curving. 'It's funny, but beautiful things often make me want to cry.'

'Yes, I know.' The kindness and affection in his clear young voice made him her friend for ever.

'What a nice little boy you are, Jon. I love you already! Now what do you think you'd like for Christmas? We'd better start planning.'

Jon's eyebrows shot up, his blue eyes lingering on her face. 'It's going to be the best Christmas ever!'

'I hope so, Jon,' Rachael said with no answering sense of hope or pleasure. Deep inside her as she looked down at his handsome little face her most complex feelings were intensifying. The blood roared in her ears, as she was confronted by the naked truth. She was in love with Nick Retford—the one thing she had never dreamed of. The bitter irony of fate! Now when she couldn't help herself, she was deeply involved. It was even possible that she wouldn't recover herself in a whole lifetime. It was a tremendous thing, this great rush of truth, and all her youth and feeling of bitter betrayal lurked in her eyes. Loving Nick Retford was like reaching for the moon. He was just as magnetic and just as much out of reach. Only one name dominated that other world. *Vanessa Maybury.*

The first evening Nick returned home, he called in briefly at the Lodge. Allie welcomed him and took him through to the drawing-room where Lady Ross and her good friend Jacob were arguing amiably over a point in cards. The card table was already set up for an evening of bridge with Allie and Maggie MacAdam, a tournament class player, to make up the numbers. Maggie as yet hadn't arrived after a day of civic duties, so the rest of them were passing the time over a few hands of poker with Jacob holding his hands over his eyes and saying wryly that he was getting old and feeble. In any case, it was always a bit difficult to beat Allie who had the right, immovable face for the game, whatever her hand.

Both of them looked up expectantly, with no doubt in their minds that it was Maggie, although she had entered with uncharacteristic quietness. If not, it could only be young Brett, who was taking Rachael out for the third evening in a row—a state of affairs Lady Ross was beginning to take exception to. For some reason Rachael was whipping herself up into a storm, super-energetic like young Jon, but so brittle and bright, something *had* to be wrong. If she didn't soon say what it was, her grandmother intended to tackle her about it. Rachael had to be helped, but it was difficult with the young; the more urgent the matter, the more inclined they were to bottle things up.

128

When Nick came into the room, they greeted him with obvious pleasure. Jacob stood up, his shrewd, mild eyes beaming, his hand extended.

'Why, hello there! What a surprise, though I didn't expect the verdict to be any different.'

'It was rather a difficult job to do all the same. How are you?' The two men shook hands and Lady Ross looked up at them, smiling.

'We're all so pleased to see you home safely again. Young Jon especially. You mean everything to him!'

There was something compellingly reassuring about his presence, the light, firm clasp of his hand. He really looked at one and acted as if he cared. Lady Ross found it immensely comforting to be engulfed by his penetrating blue gaze, admiringly and truly interested in her well-being.

'Thank you, Lady Ross.' He smiled at her, his bluer-than-blue eyes quite vivid against his tanned skin. 'I've just been up to the house. Jon's plastered me with requests. Ponies and puppies and so forth. I suspect Rachael is at the back of it!'

'From your smile I gather you think it might be a good idea.'

'Why, yes. There are a few gaps in his life I'm determined to start filling up. Thank you for being so kind to him while I've been away. He wrote a letter to me telling me all about it. Quite a good letter really.'

'I'm not surprised. He's a fine boy. You must be very proud of him.'

'I am. An area of great happiness in a sometimes lunatic world.'

Jacob silently nodded his agreement, studying the

other man and considering him an excellent prospect for some lucky woman. Mrs Maybury was all the rage. A pity! though she was rather splendid. Nick cast his glance down at the card table and came to a swift decision: 'I won't keep you from your game. I just called in to see how you were and to let you know I'm back again. I'm glad Jon wasn't too much of a nuisance. He gets very intense where his affections are involved, and I gather he's bestowed them on Rachael in an amazingly short time.'

'Yes, really something special!' Lady Ross agreed happily. 'They're good friends. Rachael should be down in a moment. She and Brett—Brett Vickers, you know—are going out again. Three evenings in a row. I hope it's not going to start an epidemic. Even young people need their rest. I swear Rachael's lost weight, but it's against the rules to protest too much. Won't you sit down, Nick?'

He shook his dark head regretfully. 'No, really, I'll call again if I may. I've still a work load to catch up on.'

'Ah, here's Rachael now!' Lady Ross said, glancing over his shoulder, her face wearing the special soft light she reserved for her granddaughter.

Rachael, arriving down the stairs, found a different audience from the one she was expecting. Hearing the murmur of voices, she had thought it was Maggie or Brett or both. Nick Retford was the last person she expected to see. Just the sight of him seemed to flay all the skin off her, her frail peace destroyed in an instant.

'Why, Nick, you're home again!' She threw up her head defensively, looking very mettlesome.

'Aren't you going to say you're pleased?' He walked

130

towards her taking her outstretched hand, his blue appraising glance leaping over her, missing nothing. 'Your grandmother's right—you have lost weight.'

'There, what did I tell you!' Allie crowed. 'All this rushing about is bad for you.'

Nick seemed to be watching her with uncanny concentration, and the warm colour over her cheekbones deepened. The door chimes pealed again, a wonderful piece of timing so far as Rachael was concerned, and Allie turned about and went to answer them. A few seconds later they heard Maggie's commanding voice followed by her very distinguished appearance, blue-grey hair, blue-grey eyes, tall and trim as a twenty-year-old, inexhaustible and always in great form.

'My darlings!' She threw out her arms towards them all. 'Ah, Mr Retford! Introduce us, Libby, at once. Dear old Jacob! Rachael, how beautiful you are, child!' She swept across the carpet, conferring honours everywhere, like a triumphant sovereign. The next few minutes were hectic, with no one daring or bothering to get over the top of Maggie, a true Leo, as forceful and as authoritative a woman as one could wish to meet, or alternatively avoid. Lady Ross, her dearest friend for sixty years, was always pleased to see her, and to a slightly lesser degree, Allie and Jacob, but Rachael couldn't relax. Maggie was being very cordial, the centre of attraction, enjoying herself enormously, thrilled to meet Nick Retford at last ... 'People say you're wonderful!' It would be such fun if he could join them ... No? Ah well, there would be many more evenings. Maggie was never beaten.

Rachael found herself breathing fast. It was a kind

of ordeal being so close to Nick, but it wouldn't be for long. Brett should arrive soon to rescue her. At that stage, Nick looked down at her, staring right into the depths of her eyes, trying to fathom just what made her tick. 'Why are you so nervous?' he asked softly.

'N-nonsense!' She stammered a little, which was both dangerous and damning.

'It's true. Are we back to square one?'

'You tell me.'

'Rachael, you've done it again!' His white smile was terse.

Irresistibly her eyes clung to him, and that would be the snag. She would have to avoid him altogether to develop any kind of immunity. There was a curious brilliant intimacy in his gaze. She couldn't for the life of her sustain it with Maggie looking on so avidly, though it was as well she had arrived, carrying all before her.

But for once that state of affairs was to be corrected. Somehow, as unobtrusively as possible, Maggie found herself being stage-managed. With all the courtesies observed, the bridge party found itself under way and Rachael herself out in the night air with Nick at her elbow waiting with her until such time as her escort would drive in through the front gates, a minute or so hence.

'You've been up to the house, of course?' she was driven to polite conversation.

'Yes, I've seen Jon.' His glance was half amused, half irritated as though her stilted manner annoyed him. Her breath caught and she turned away with a kind of urgency.

132

'No wonder you love him.'

'I'm trying to like *you*, Rachael!' he pointed out rather crisply. 'Is there something I've done or omitted to do?'

'Don't be absurd!' she said crossly.

'You're obviously disturbed about something. Frightened, maybe!'

'I don't have to defend myself, Nick. How was your trip to Adelaide?'

'It was in all the papers.'

'It's not the professional side I'm inquiring about.'

'Really? Do I have to answer for anything else?'

Used as she had become to Brett's earnest, adoring face, she found Nick too darkly, vividly masculine, a mature man prepared to put her well and truly in her place. It made no sense at all to court danger deliberately. She moved swiftly back into the pool of light, the lamp flashing out the ruby tints in her hair. The scent of the roses was almost unbearable. Life was full of heartbreak and there were worse things in store for her.

He looked at his watch, then glanced at her very coolly. 'That is a beautiful dress.'

'I just hope Brett likes it!' she said, putting it a bit strongly. 'It's his favourite colour.'

'Which one? It seems to be a swirl of them. I don't know why you bother. He thinks you're perfect anyway.'

'I wish he would come!' she said, trembling visibly. She was suffering and he was the cause of it. She could *hit* him!

'What's wrong with you?' Abruptly his hands came

133

up and covered her shoulders. 'Why this terrific build-up of tension? At the very least I expected just ordinary behaviour.'

'I can never, never be myself with you, Nick.'

'You mean you won't let yourself be! I thought we'd signed a cease-fire. The last time I saw you, you seemed utterly carefree, now you're back to the first hostility. In God's name, why?'

'There's no explaining reactions, Nick. Perhaps I don't know my own mind.'

'I've decided that.' There was an odd little twist to his mouth and with shock she realised that he was jaded and moody and she was the cause of it. Her slender body was poised warily, the constraint tangible between them. Met on all sides by love from her childhood as she had been, this alien, sexual antagonism was too much for her. He thought badly of her—it was apparent in the sternness of his face. The night was beautiful nevertheless, the moon and the flowers, the white jasmine, making it difficult to be sensible. How unhappy she was! She was nearly shrinking inside.

'Oh, it's Brett!' she stammered thankfully.

'You *are* pleased!' he said very curtly indeed.

'Well, you're not in a gentle mood. Are you going to say hello?'

'I think I've exhausted my supply of goodwill. Thank you for watching over Jon. I appreciate that.'

'Please, Nick . . .' she begged.

'Please, Nick, what?'

His skin in the light gleamed like dark copper, but his eyes had an icy sheen. Incredibly he was angry about something. She was acting strangely, she knew that, but *he* was the one with the split personality, wanting to charm every woman he met, his background paved with success. What had he expected? She couldn't go straight into his arms, which was what she desperately wanted, and was going to a great deal of trouble to conceal.

'I'm sorry if I've disappointed you in some way,' she found herself saying.

His expression seemed to relent a little. 'Oh well, I should be used to it. You're obviously determined to sell your friendship dearly.'

'Why should you want it?'

He just shrugged, looking down at her intently, her creamy skin, the dark red mane of hair, her eyes brilliant in the lamplight. 'You're beautiful, Rachael,' he said slowly. 'Frightfully spoilt, of course, but the most incredible part is you're still a child. It's as well I see you the way you really are.'

'And you think you're perfect?' she demanded.

'Only in some things. Don't claw at me, little one, your friend Brett is looking quite anxious. I'm sure you don't want to dampen his evening.'

'Brett's friendship is very important to me,' she said, almost tearfully.

Nick's dark, disturbing voice was laced with self-mockery. 'Oh, why, oh, why did I start this conversation? Go along and enjoy yourself. I'm burning to get back to the house. Which reminds me, do you think Jon should have a pony and a puppy and anything else that occurs to you?'

'Indeed I do! I'd ask him first if he wants a stepmother, though!'

An iron grip locked her wrist. 'You can't skip that! What does it mean?'

'Sorry, Nick!' She tried to shake free of him. 'Our time's up. Besides, I'm sure you've already thought of a name.'

'I hardly see that as your business.'

'Oh, go to the devil!' she snapped, trying to get the last word.

He released her abruptly. 'Run, Rachael, but you're simply going to pay for that one.'

'All I want is for you to leave me alone!' she said, lifting her eyes to him.

'As a matter of fact, I might prefer that myself.'

'Good. I'm delighted. I hope you live happily ever after. You will let me see Jon?'

'Such a pathetic plea. Why should I?'

'Because he's my friend.'

'You're going to have to do better than that, Rachael.'

'I care about him,' she said as if she were at the end of her tether.

'That's fine.'

'I certainly don't care about you,' she cried, her eyes flashing with all the old fire.

'No secret. Do you think your thoughts transparent? Young Vickers is more your type. See what you can do about it.'

'You're furious, but I don't have to put up with it.'

'Whatever's in store for you, Rachael, you'll richly deserve.'

'Oh? It's a good thing it's not your mission in life.'

'It would give me some satisfaction, however. You

believe you can't wait to get away from me. Why don't you go?'

Determinedly, as if to add new evidence to the totality of his disgust with her, Nick walked quickly away, lifting an acknowledging hand to the slightly baffled Brett. He swung into his car and was moving it up the drive within seconds. Rachael hesitated a moment, trying to shake his image from her. Good or bad, Nick was to haunt her. She felt faint with the pain of it, a look of strain on her face. She would have to go carefully with Nick. He wasn't the man to tolerate her all too evident complications, but they were easier than letting him discover she had fallen in love with him.

With a considerable effort she ran to Brett's car, trying to speak gaily. 'Hello there! You're late.'

Brett checked his watch. 'Maybe five minutes. The traffic was bad. Nick's back, I see.'

'Oh, don't let's talk about Nick Retford. He doesn't exist for us.' She slid into the bucket seat, pushing her hair back, her eyes glittery, a high colour over her cheekbones.

'What is it?' asked Brett in some consternation. 'You look as if you've got a fever.'

'Too much blusher.'

'That's your own colour. Feel all right?'

'Do I meet with your approval or not?'

Slanted amber eyes met his with a decided challenge, her gleaming red hair brushed back from her brow. She presented a very imperious picture, her slender throat rising from the deep V neckline of her dress. Brett stared at her, then began to laugh.

'Let's go. *Immediately!*'

'Sally and Dave coming?' she asked.

'Yes, and a few others. I'm glad she dropped that Craig. He bored me to the point of tears.'

'He asked me out.'

'What did you say?' queried Brett.

'I said you and I were practically engaged, old buddy.'

'You've no idea how much I want it.'

'Excuse me, don't talk engagements,' she said hastily.

'No. Your twenty-first birthday would be a good time to make an announcement.'

'Are you deaf, Brett?' Rachael demanded crossly.

'Well, I inhaled a good deal of night air waiting for you to come to the car. We both know Nick Retford disturbs you in some way.'

'And nothing to be done about it. Perhaps it will clear up when he's married. I hear it settles a man.'

'Who's he marrying?' asked Brett.

'Vanessa Maybury.'

'Rugged!'

'I don't understand why you say that. She's a very good-looking woman and I understand she's quite witty and well connected and so forth.'

'To be sure. But they didn't look deeply involved to me.'

'I can't go into details, my friend, but I have it on excellent authority that they're to be married.'

'Ah well, these affairs lead to something!' Brett turned to bestow on her his irrepressible smile. 'Even our childhood friendship can't remain static. Tonight I'm going to sweep you off your feet. I promise!'

CHAPTER SIX

RACHAEL went through to the rear terrace as Dino suggested. It was a hot, still day and the tiny plot of land at the back of the coffee shop was extraordinarily green and restful. Besides, Dino's coffee was excellent, as were the numerous little Italian delicacies that went with it, sweet or savoury, or perhaps sandwiches, filled to perfection and garnished with the lettuce or fresh sprigs of parsley that grew in the herb borders directly behind her. Dino's was the place to relax and ease some of the midday tensions. Right at that moment Dino was coming to her aid with a tray of his own selection. He knew her tastes in any case and the coffee shop was rapidly filling.

'There!' He deposited the tray on the table and began removing the few items one by one, placing them before her. 'Don't I prove to you you are one of my favourites?'

'Thank you, Dino,' she said gratefully. 'You're a true friend. How's Connie and the children?'

He shook his head, smiling. 'Must you always remind me I'm a married man?'

'You couldn't be anything else, Dino. Your contentment shows. Such beautiful children you have, and Connie always so happy!'

Dino widened his magnificent dark eyes. '*Mamma mia*, you should have seen her this morning! In a rage, like Vesuvius, quite frightening! But what is this with you?' he asked gently, kindness and much perception in his darkly olive-skinned face.

Rachael looked up in surprise. 'Why, nothing, Dino. I'm just a little tired. I've been discussing career prospects for most of the morning, then I had a few errands to attend to for Gran.'

'And how is your so beautiful *nonna*?' he asked in his normal manner.

'The same, Dino. Gran's a rare woman.'

'I admire her extravagantly!' Dino maintained, not content to leave it there but kissing his fingertips. 'She has the most amazing personality. When she first started to come to my little café I was honoured. I was made.'

'Now we all come because there isn't a more pleasant place to have a cup of coffee anywhere. You see to people individually, you and Connie. I wouldn't think of going anywhere else.'

'Please never cease to repeat this to your friends. Now you sit there, *piccola*, and breathe in the fresh air. You look a little pale. You'll have to convince me there's nothing wrong before you go. Remember I am your father confessor!'

'More or less, Dino,' she smiled.

As he moved back through the sliding glass doorway, a flow of customers spilled out on to the terrace with its circular tables covered in crisp sun-yellow linen and shaded by multi-striped white-fringed umbrellas. There were a lot of carefree *ciao*'s and hi's and a little joke from Dino, then the tables started to fill up. Rachael paid no attention to the changing scene around her. She just wanted to sit quietly in peace, too unhappy these days to really know what was happening to her. She sipped at her coffee, congratulating herself she was to be left alone for a while at least, when a familiar, rather clipped voice assailed her ear:

'Why, hello there, Miss Ross. How nice to see you. May I join you?'

Dear God, Rachael thought in desperation, what next? She looked up, doing her best to summon up a welcoming smile. 'Mrs Maybury, how are you? Yes, certainly sit down.'

'How lucky I am to have seen you, and it's *Vanessa*, please. After all, that Mrs Maybury is soon to be changed!' As immaculate as ever in white with a neat little hat to match the beautiful silk scarf at her throat, Vanessa slid elegantly into the chair opposite. 'Really, this place is delightful!' She gazed about her with every appearance of pleasure.

'Do you come here often?' Rachael asked.

'Actually, no. This is my first visit, but it confirms what my friends tell me. What are you having? Um, that looks delicious. I'll have the same, though I shouldn't. I watch my figure.'

Vanessa turned rather sharply and gestured imperiously towards the briskly circling Dino, whose jaw fell open at this impersonation of a pitiless Roman Empress.

'*Scusi*, Signora,' he responded with masterly calm, 'one moment and I shall be at your service. Felice!' He waved over his head to his very dapper young assistant, 'attend to the Signora, if you please.' Dino over the years had become a little spoilt by his own success and he rarely encountered the painful arrogance the tall blonde lady was displaying. A man of great natural courtesy himself, he found such arbitrary behaviour jarring. The lady was very good-looking, certainly, but waxy like a doll with a painted, immobile face. Little Rachael beside her wore an expression that told him plainly she wasn't overjoyed by the sudden arrival of this handsome haughty person. In fact Dino decided he didn't want to see her again if she couldn't act sweetly as a woman should. He was no humble peasant but a café owner. Really! ... It hurt him, such insensitivity. He turned back to his customer Mrs Edwards and completed her order. Her sympathetic smile made him recover his usual sunny nature.

Vanessa, meanwhile, gave her order to the respectful Felice very clearly and distinctly as though he might be an idiot or with only one or two words of English at his command. Felice, born in Australia of migrant parents, bore it and was dismissed with a meaningless smile for his trouble.

'I was supposed to meet Nick today,' Vanessa confided, 'but something came up at the last minute. It always does. He never seems to have a moment to himself, but I'll have to get used to it. He's certainly good value when I do see him. How are you settling down at the Lodge? You don't find the situation awkward?'

'Only the question. In what way do you mean?'

'Why, surely ...!' Vanessa gave a little embarrassed laugh. 'The change in your circumstances, dear. It would really worry me.'

'You don't give that impression,' said Rachael. 'You look a very cool person to me.'

'I suppose I am. Allow me to beg your indulgence for a few minutes. Do you mind if I smoke?'

Rachael shook her head. A non-smoker herself, she really detested it. Vanessa, however, was only going through the formalities. She had every intention of smoking. She selected a cigarette carefully, lit it and took a long appreciative draw. 'I imagine in time you'll start hunting for something more suitable?'

Rachael ignored the slightly metallic crispness, keeping her face bland. 'My grandmother is nearly eighty, Mrs Maybury. The lease will run for the remainder of her lifetime. She's quite happy at the Lodge. It suits her. Mr Retford actually suggested the whole thing.'

'That sounds like Nick! But really, Miss Ross ...' Vanessa looked more and more pained. 'You must understand, I don't want to upset you in any way. It's really rather delicate and I'd be grateful ...'

'Could I get you to the point?' Rachael interrupted. 'Are you suggesting we move out?'

'Since you put it that way, after Nick and I are married I *would* like the place to myself. Surely that's understandable?'

'Yes, it is. We didn't realise your marriage was so imminent.'

'Oh, I've made up my mind irrevocably,' Vanessa said.

'Has Nick?' Rachael's throat felt parched and she sipped at her coffee.

'Oh, please!' Vanessa shrugged off such a stupid, impertinent question. 'Understand the position immediately, Miss Ross. You must have known Nick and I would eventually get married.'

'I can't see how that would alter anything,' Rachael looked down at her cup. 'We would all have to go right out of our way to see each other. In the ordinary way we wouldn't even be considered near neighbours. Ten acres is generally considered to be a good amount of space, and the Lodge is screened off completely from the rest of the estate. Of course we could collide coming in the front gate. Is that what's bothering you?'

Vanessa sat still for a moment, her cigarette suspended in mid-air. 'I can see I'm upsetting you. I'm sorry. I just never dreamed you'd want to stay on after we were married.'

'And when is this happy event to be?' Rachael asked, a hard constriction round her chest.

'Now, now,' Vanessa said playfully. 'I can't give away secrets. Nick doesn't want any fuss. He's a very private person in so far as he can be, but I might just let slip it will be early in the New Year.'

The words seemed to come at a rush. 'How do you get on with Jon?' asked Rachael.

'Extremely well. He's an exceptional child. He realises his father must marry again. No doubt he'll be going to a really good boarding school before long.'

'That's not what his father told me.'

'Perhaps you misunderstood him?' Vanessa smiled, rather tightly. She really did have a thin mouth, but it was beautifully painted beyond the natural outline.

'No,' Rachael said slowly. 'I can't help wondering if *you* did.'

Colour began to mount in Vanessa's long throat and she deserted the dignified approach. 'It's repugnant to

144

me to mention this,' she said with obvious relish, 'but haven't you a first-class crush on Nick?'

'Does anything about me suggest I have?'

Vanessa laughed bitterly. 'Nick's a very experienced man. He's handsome and wealthy and he's at the top of his profession—an irresistible combination of qualities. How many girls in your position wouldn't imagine themselves in love with him?'

'He mightn't be everyone's cup of tea,' Rachael said with a semblance of calm. 'I do believe I'm stunned at this conversation.'

'I don't see why!' Vanessa said stridently. 'I've hesitated before mentioning any of this. I didn't want to interfere directly . . .'

'You're interfering all right!' Rachael broke in on her.

'Well, you must have been expecting it. I'm not the woman to let the grass grow under her feet.'

'Obviously not, which brings me to a question. Did you follow me?'

'Only because I had to. I'm very methodical, Miss Ross, and I guard my interests.'

'I understand.'

'Now I find myself face to face with a slight dilemma. I know I can rely on your discretion. The important thing is that we women keep it to ourselves. I think it perfectly natural I should want Swans' Reach to myself.'

'*You* should, for heaven's sake!'

Vanessa rummaged for another cigarette. 'Once I'm Nick's wife,' she said curtly, 'regardless of your feelings or those of your grandmother, I would want you out!

I'm no fool, Miss Ross, don't think I am. I know quite well you're attracted to Nick. He's taken you out to dinner ...'

'So?'

'So all women in love have a sixth sense. You can see for yourself I don't care for Nick to be paying you any attention.'

'I think he was just being kind.'

'Very likely. I know Nick. Normally I would fully support him in these charitable gestures, but as I've already said, young girls are very unpredictable, and you do have a pretty face. One can't very well have such complications right on the fence, so to speak.'

'Why so afraid of me, Mrs Maybury?'

'My dear, I'm *not*!' Vanessa muttered. 'I'm sympathetic. Most of my friends are attracted to Nick, but mercifully they're all married. You can end up badly hurt. Believe me, my dear, I'm speaking in absolute sincerity. Isn't there somewhere else you could go? A luxury apartment perhaps. I understand you're still very well off by ordinary standards.'

'Who told you that?'

'Why, Nick, my dear. Who else?'

'We're comfortable, Mrs Maybury,' Rachael replied drily, 'and we're not getting out of the Lodge. Not until such time as my grandmother expresses the desire to leave, and I would strongly advise you not to have any conversation with her on this score. I won't have her upset and neither, I am certain, will Nick Retford. You don't look it, but you're obviously a very jealous woman. I represent no threat to you or your plans.'

'I hope not, for your sake,' Vanessa said tightly. 'I

can be a formidable enemy, my dear, and I don't let anything get in my way!'

'Do you lie as well?'

Vanessa's hand trembled violently. 'I won't be insulted by a love-struck teenager!'

'I'm almost twenty-one.'

'The right age for a crush on an older man. I do believe I suffered a bad case of it myself at one time.'

'Did you marry your fixation?' asked Rachael coldly.

'Of course not. My late husband didn't attract me in that way.'

'Good heavens, no wonder you have no children.'

'I confess I'm not deeply maternal, Miss Ross. A lot of women aren't, you know. It does get rather forced on one.'

'Jon, I believe, would love a brother to share all his fun.'

'That doesn't perturb me. At my age I don't propose to embark on childbirth and all its attendant glories, not that it has anything remotely to do with you.'

'I apologise.'

Vanessa laughed, receiving her order with a belated show of enthusiasm and civility. Probably she was hungry after delivering herself of her chosen message. 'Have another coffee, Miss Ross,' she said brightly, 'and let's make peace!'

'I wasn't aware we were at war, because basically I don't want to fight anybody.'

'Yes, there's also the reason that you might be beaten.'

'I'm sure you are more than a match for me.'

'Experience, my dear!' Vanessa drawled.

'No. Inclination. I'll never be any different. I give up immediately. I even see all hostility as futile and ugly.'

'Then keep this between the two of us, like a sensible girl. After all, I had to make my position clear, didn't I?'

'If everything is going so well, Mrs Maybury, may I ask why?' said Rachael.

'Sometimes if one nips symptoms in the bud, they can't develop into anything incurable, if you know what I mean.'

'I'm against 'flu injections myself.'

'Oh, don't be tiresome! You know what I mean, you're not a baby. You might even consider that a man like Nick might become embarrassed if you insist on complicating the arrangements he's made.'

'Which you are apparently trying to alter. Have you checked with him first? I wouldn't care to cross him myself. It would be very difficult to embarrass Nick Retford. I'd call him totally impervious.'

'Why, you're not leaving?' Vanessa stared at her in mock astonishment.

Rachael stood up, gathering her things. 'I must, regardless of what fun you're having.'

'Ah well,' Vanessa looked down again, and stirred her coffee. 'You're at the age to take offence easily.'

'And you're at the age to leave that last bit of cheesecake alone. It's better than dieting for two days.'

Rachael moved quickly away from the table, realising her last remark was a little bit childish and it wasn't really her style, but Vanessa seemed blind to all but the most personal insults. It was bad enough to lose her home, but to have it go to Vanessa Maybury was

148

an outrage. She drew in her breath, feeling as though she was badly scarred for the rest of her life. In spite of Vanessa's efforts to ridicule her 'crush' on Nick (what a deplorable word) Vanessa had not been successful in concealing her own anxieties.

Nick's dark face was etched in her brain. She hadn't spoken to him for days and it affected her beyond belief. She had even passed his car coming on to the highway and he hadn't acknowledged her in any way, not even the brusque little wave of her hand. To use Allie's phrase, she was 'on the outer' with Nick. By the time she got home, Allie had gone into the village to shop and her grandmother's bedroom door was closed, which meant she was resting. Gran never did like the hot summer months, which sapped her energy.

Rachael took off her chic city clothes and reached for a pair of linen shorts and a matching halter top. The heat was intense. Since the Neil Diamond concert that had drawn a crowd of thirty-eight thousand, he had become quite a favourite of hers. She took her portable record player and a pile of new recordings and went down to the shady side of the house near the sparkling river. The magnificent shade trees, planted a century before, seemed doubly attractive in the shimmering heat, the scent of the frangipani in that section of the garden all-pervading.

She lay in the freshly mown grass and listened to the lyrics. In the light of her own feelings they seemed to take on a fresh meaning.

Song sung blue, everybody's got one . . .

This was her language. It was part of the human condition to fall in and out of love. Love was a basic essen-

149

tial of life like food and drink. As it was, she was starving. She closed her eyes in the perfumed haze, wanting and wanting what the songs put a name to. They were making her sad, rising and falling, tremulous too, yearning ... A few seconds later something flicked across her face and landed near her ear. A creamy, yellow-centred frangipani blossom. She opened her eyes to her biggest shock of the day—all six feet of him, elegant and mocking, brilliant eyes aware of the picture she made, the flawless young limbs, and the youthful abandon. The biggest trespasser of them all, Nick.

'This is a surprise!' she said faintly.

'How formal. Shall we shake hands?' His voice had a dry measuring note to it. 'Is it possible to look cool and exotic at once?'

'Words, Nick,' she retaliated, her eyes golden in the subdued light, 'you don't sound as if you mean them.'

'Maybe I don't!' He glanced down at the glossy record covers. 'Neil Diamond. Did you go to his concert?'

'Yes, I did. About forty of us made up a party. It was great. Do you like him?'

'Yes, I do. He's different. He's got talent.'

'Are you going to sit down or are you just going to stand there?'

'Staring at you, you mean?'

'I didn't say that, Nick. I'm sorry for what happened the last time I saw you.'

'What *did* happen?' he asked as if he hadn't the faintest recollection.

'Oh, forget it,' she said with a pretence of carelessness. 'It's too hot to argue.'

'I daresay, but we don't seem able to help it.' He lowered his lean frame to the grass beside her.

'How's Jon?' she asked.

'He's fine. I pick him up in an hour.'

'You don't usually have the afternoon off.'

'I don't usually work so damned hard,' he answered abruptly.

'Sorry, Mr Retford.' Rachael went to reach back. 'Shall I turn off the record player?'

'No, don't bother. I like it. I think I might even pull your hair. Beautiful,' he said.

She made a funny little sound, feeling she was submerging under a great ocean wave. What did it really mean to him that he was going to marry Vanessa Maybury? Everyone knew. She should be running furiously over the grass to the safety of the house, but she also knew she was going to stay right where she was, for all the danger signals. She jerked her head a little away from him, a token gesture, but with a strand of her hair twisted around his finger it hurt her.

'Ouch!' The husky little cry was torn from her.

'You deserve it.'

'Thank you.' She tried to invest it with outrage, but she was, and sounded, physically breathless. This was a fantasy, the heat and the flowers, Nick there beside her, somehow materialising to the tumultuous beat of the music. What was it, black magic? If it was, it was urgent. In another minute she would be out of control. He aroused an irresistible need in her that he should never have started. He was the mature one, the experienced one. She was alarmed at her own vulnerability. If this was love, it was shocking, a wordless anguish.

'Well, what's the verdict?' Turquoise eyes slashed at her.

'No further questions!'

'Well, *I* have . What are you thinking about?'

'It might surprise you.'

'I don't think so.'

'Don't incite me, Nick!' She turned on him, her eyes smouldering. 'I haven't your level of sophistication.'

'I'm sorry to tell you I'm not even rising to it myself. It must be the heat.'

The mockery in his voice startled her. Rachael risked another glance at him, seeking vainly to know his mind. His blue eyes were so clear and sparkling one would have thought they reached through to his soul, his hair ebony-black with no trace of brown in it. Nick, the enigma! For something to do she picked up her sunglasses, but he took them out of her nerveless fingers and dropped them on the grass again.

'I want to look at you, Rachael. Not coloured glass.'

'I find myself surprised!' she said wryly. 'A lot of things don't seem to be right!'

'At least we know what it *is*. I'm giving a party Saturday night, a kind of house-warming. I want you to come.'

A pain sharpened and moved in her breast. Not in a million years, with Vanessa Maybury the Queen Bee! 'I don't think so, Nick,' she said, slightly averting her head.

'Why not?' He stared at her for a few seconds, his

anger rising. 'Such a slender young creature to be so unyielding. You should be middle-aged with a stubborn chin!'

She almost groaned. 'I'm doing my best, Nick, but I don't want to come to the party. You and your friends don't need me. Mrs Maybury, I'm sure, will give you all the support you need.'

'Support! Who the hell mentioned support?' he asked with a kind of cold anger. 'You fascinate me, Rachael, you really do.'

'And in such a short time. I'm worrying about it.'

'We'll return to that later. *Now* I want you to tell me you're coming.'

'Surely you don't think I'd enjoy it?' Rachael demanded incredulously.

'There is a possibility, surely?'

'No, and that's final!'

'What if I persuade you?' His blue eyes narrowed over her.

'I'm adamant.'

'Yes, that generally describes you, that and a few other terms, but don't you see, I'm just not going to accept it.'

'You'll have to!' she said recklessly. 'You can't order me about!'

'Ever heard of brute force?'

'You wouldn't use it.'

'Wouldn't I! A little bit of it is better for you than you know.'

'That's obvious!' Somehow she was on her back in the grass staring up at him, her arms locked on either side, her skin stretched taut with a deep consciousness.

'Don't worry,' he said rather drily, 'I'm not going to ruin your young life. You just keep perfectly still.'

She made a strangled little sound and tried to turn her head. 'It isn't as though the place is swarming with people.'

'Even that as an appeal wouldn't be very effective. You insist on backing yourself into tight corners.'

'And you're trouble, for sure,' she said, her voice shaking.

'Sometimes trouble is good for you, Rachael.'

There were strange leaping lights in his eyes, and his face had a hard, disturbing charm that unnerved her. 'I thought you were too clever, Nick, to create situations you don't want or need.'

'What man is *too* clever?' he asked lightly.

She fixed him with a look of extreme temperament, intensified by her physical helplessness. 'You're being extremely inconsiderate, making more problems for me.'

He shook his dark head. 'My mind can't be functioning as well as you think. What are you talking about?' He was laughing under his breath, a saturnine cast to his face.

'Are you going to kiss me or not?' she said, her eyes flashing.

'Yes, damn it, I am. It's the best way to deal with you!'

She reacted like a small wildcat, twisting and trying to hit out with fervour. Nick was outrageous, treating her as though she was the very least of his worries, yet he was breaking her resistance without disturbing his breath:

'Rachael, stop it!'

'Oh, damn!' She turned up her face, his power over her much too profound.

He slid his arms under her back, pulling her against his chest. 'Promise you'll come!'

'No!'

'Bravado.'

The kiss was sufficient, making her yield without being aware she was doing it on purpose. She was vaguely aware of her hand in his hair, then against the side of his face, the skin polished with the faintest, tantalising rasp. He murmured something to her that she could not hear. This was a miracle. She truly believed it. The most beautiful cascade of feeling, so perfect she didn't have any right to it. She had no pride either, for he was kissing her as though he would never let her go. It was unabashed double dealing! She fought away from that shattering, deceitful mouth:

'Just a minute!'

He laughed and went to pull her back against him, his blue eyes so flaring and brilliant she almost fell to the ground again, if only for a minute so that he would kiss her again.

'What is it?' he was still laughing.

Rachael held up her face to the scented breeze, wishing she could tell him, but she knew perfectly well that Vanessa Maybury could be vengeful. 'When are you getting married, Nick?' she asked heavily.

He put out a hand and encircled her bare ankle. 'Guess.'

'The New Year, I've been told.'

'Then the New Year it is.'

'You rotten beast!'

'Don't talk like Jon,' he scolded. 'You're almost a woman.'

'Not woman enough for you.'

'Do you want to be?' he asked.

'Of course not. You're for ever doing things you shouldn't.'

'Yes indeed. Would you please come to my party, Rachael, as a very special favour?'

'Perhaps for an hour,' she relented.

'I'll bet you stay longer.'

She shrugged, as if even if it were true, it made no difference. She was still doing him a favour. 'Can I come with you when you pick up Jon?'

'I was just going to ask you. I know you're only being kind to me for his sake.'

'Damn you, Nick!' she exclaimed furiously, but he only took her hand, drawing her up beside him, seeing through the shower of sparks she thought would protect her from him.

'Did you love your wife, Nick?'

'Is this going to be a serious conversation?'

'That depends on you. You don't have to answer me if you don't want to. You can even tell me to mind my own business. I understand some things.'

'Yes, Rachael, I loved my wife. I would never have married her in the first place if I hadn't. In that respect I'm surprised you asked. You don't really think I'd go around marrying women I don't love?'

'No, of course not. I'm sorry.' She did in fact sound very young and contrite. 'Poor little Jon. Poor you. I've never felt sorry for you before.'

'I know that! And you don't have to feel sorry for me now. There are different kinds of loving. Different degrees.'

I love you, she thought so intensely, it might have been a brand on her forehead. As she thought of Nick and the young wife he had lost, her heart twisted with pain. The sadness and grief he had known. She really didn't know him at all. She couldn't even guess at what he had been through. He was a wonderful father to Jon, who adored him, and it couldn't have been easy managing a child and a brilliant rising career.

Her fingers twined through his of her own accord, and he looked down at her glowing head with something very like tenderness in his blue eyes. 'I can tell you something, Rachael, and maybe it's a disloyalty to Anne's little ghost, I don't know ... but I've never felt for a woman what I know I *can*. Up until now.'

'Then you'd better get married, Nick!' she said, sadly renouncing him.

'Come to my wedding?'

'No.'

'You'll change your mind,' he assured her.

Heaven protect her! By then she would have to be far away from Swans' Reach, even if she had to shift Gran. Vanessa, it seemed, was to have all her wishes granted. Nick, beside her, studied her quiet face, but whatever he was thinking he kept to himself.

CHAPTER SEVEN

'You look beautiful, Rachael!' said Lady Ross, scrutinising her granddaughter with a critical eye. 'But there's something in your face that bothers me, a little reckless light. It reminds me of Dirk.'

'What's wrong with looking like my father?'

'Turn round.'

Rachael did so, pirouetting slightly, so that her chiffon skirt floated out about her. 'I'm going to a party, yet it seems like a battlefield,' she confessed.

'What a very strange thing to say!'

'Mrs Maybury will be there,' Rachael supplied, as if that answered everything.

'So?' her grandmother asked, after a moment's consideration.

'So Mrs Maybury doesn't like me.'

'Is that important, darling? Nick obviously does.'

'Why does Nick like me?'

'Oh, Rachael!' Her grandmother gave a truly Gallic gesture. 'He'd have a hard time not liking you.'

'I love him.'

'I know that,' her grandmother said softly.

'Then what am I going to do about it, Gran? You're the oracle.'

'Well, my powers are somewhat depleted, but I'd advise you to sit still and wait.'

'What, for a wedding! Nick's and Vanessa Maybury's? What a nightmare.'

Her grandmother just looked at her. 'I think if I've learned anything at all, Rachael, it's that the most carefully laid plans go astray.'

'I'm sorry, Gran.' Rachael put her arms around her grandmother and hugged her. 'But Mrs Maybury told me she and Nick were getting married in the New Year.'

'Strange that Nick hasn't mentioned it, and I was only speaking to him yesterday.'

'You really like him, don't you, Gran?'

'He makes me feel young again, so I can well imagine his effect on you.'

'Perhaps it's a crush?' Rachael turned back to the mirror to examine her face.

'Perhaps it is,' her grandmother said lightly. 'Time will tell. Are you going to wear my pendant?'

'Yes, thank you. You know, I couldn't stay here if it happened, Gran.'

'Let's take each hurdle as it comes. We've been doing quite well lately. Even at eighty one can grow another skin. Actually dear old Mag suggested a boat trip.'

'At seventy-eight?' Rachael whirled round in surprise.

'I'm seventy-nine, Rachael, and I'd be keen to go. I haven't seen London or Paris in years, let alone Canada or the United States. I thought we might all go. Allie as well. She's been so good to us I'd like to reward her. Not when I'm dead and gone but *now*. Maggie thinks a trip might be just the answer. You know how she loves company and travelling.'

'I can foresee a trickling exodus into the sea,' said Rachael drily.

'Don't be silly, darling, Maggie is very much admired. She had lots and lots of admirers when she was younger.'

'That's just what I mean. Sometimes Maggie forgets she's seventy-eight. Well, at least Allie would be there to look after you.'

'Maggie is very efficient as well, dear.'

'She's not Allie, Gran. Allie knows when to call a halt. You *are* a dark horse.'

'I know, and I love my little girl. Think about it, darling. There's always an escape route. Now, when you go up to the house, kindly remember who you are.'

'And who am I?' Rachael laughed.

Her grandmother, however, was quite serious. 'You're a Ross, dear. That means you must conduct yourself accordingly. Don't do anything impulsive, and do steer clear of Mrs Maybury. After all, it's for your own good. I know you're going to have a lovely time. Nick will see to it.'

The telephone rang in the hallway and a moment later Allie came up the stairs and along to Rachael's bedroom. 'That was Nick. He said he'd pick you up in five minutes.'

'That was nice of him,' Lady Ross said complacently.

'He doesn't have to leave his own party to do that!' Rachael protested. 'I told him I'd walk.'

'Obviously he wants to take you himself, kiddo!'

'I'm not shy,' Rachael maintained.

'We knew that long ago, dearie.'

'Well, Allie, what do you think?'

'You look like a canna lily. What a trick to match up your dress with your eyes. Only two people I've ever known have had your colour eyes.'

'That's the way of it!' Lady Ross smiled. 'Lew used to call them "Cleopatra's eyes".'

'No use arguing with that one!' Allie circled Rachael's standing figure, looking for any possible flaw, but could find none. 'I wish I could go with you,' she said wistfully.

'I promised Nick we'd go up to the house over Christmas, Allie,' Lady Ross said. 'I'll feel better by then. He tells me he's made a few changes that I'll be interested to see. He's a man of great sensibility, Nick.'

Rachael gave a faint smile. 'Well, he can't do anything wrong in your eyes, Gran.'

'I knew that the moment I met him. If we had to lose our home at least it's to a man I feel I know and understand. Swans' Reach is in good hands.'

'Nevertheless, it's ironic,' Rachael said slowly. 'Remember how much I opposed him?'

'Do we ever!' Allie snorted. 'You ought to learn something from that.'

'Some lessons are salutary, some can be hell.'

'Now, now, Rachael, you're going to enjoy yourself. Take that expression off your face, it troubles me.'

'How's that?' Rachael gave her familiar, heart-stopping smile.

'Beautiful, dear!'

'I cannot but agree,' Allie said extravagantly. 'Don't worry, kid, I'm always on your side.'

Rachael's first reaction when she saw Nick was that her love for him must be blazing all over her. She couldn't, after all, tell him, so she acted out almost the reverse. He didn't seem to see anything peculiar in this, for his blue glance made her go weak at the knees. The house was a blaze of lights, like a ship at sea in the soft purple darkness. For a second only her skin went icy, because she loved it and her whole life had been altered. Nick eased the big car into the garage and turned off the ignition.

'Ready? I won't tell you how beautiful you look. There will be plenty of others to do that.'

'Nevertheless I'd like to hear it from you.'

He held her chin and inspected her face. 'You remind me of any number of flowers. Roses, tulips, lilies, it all depends what you wear.'

'That's nice enough, Nick. No wonder my grandmother's in love with you.'

'And that's bad?'

'No. I'm pleased. I really am.'

'And what about you?' asked Nick. 'A few months ago to my certain knowledge you were nursing a violent hate.'

'Yes, it even surprised me.'

'And now?'

'Don't try to turn my head. It's no good for you to try.'

'To be a success, Rachael,' he said lightly, 'one has to overcome challenges!'

'This one won't be easy.'

'Really?' He came round to her and helped her out

of the car. 'You're only pretending to be so serious, you're trembling.'

'I didn't say I didn't enjoy your company, Nick. I just expect you to act responsibly.'

'What a struggle when you look so magical.'

'Shall we go up?' she said.

'Certainly. I think you'll approve of my friends. I find them pretty interesting myself.'

'Are they all from the law world?'

'Good lord, no, but none of them are struggling. Come and see!'

Upstairs, the big reception rooms of the house had been redecorated in a different, perhaps more vital style than that of Rachael's grandfather's time. The traditional had gained a new dimension, for several of the most beautiful pieces of furniture were original to the house, the great chandeliers remained, but the inspiration was essentially very modern, the more formal ambience giving way to function and comfort and a perfect balance of the old and the new. Rachael looked around swiftly, and found absolutely nothing to criticise. Without her grandfather's gorgeous clutter the rooms looked bigger than ever, and they were ideal for large parties. The wallpaper had been changed and it toned beautifully with the existing carpet, but where the original colour scheme had been muted, it now sang, the crimson of the beautiful area rug in front of the fireplace illuminating the gold carpet and repeated in the motif of the drapery. The new sofas that faced one another across an oriental coffee table were upholstered in gold velvet, and the rest of the pieces, the ornaments and paintings were in excellent taste. Coming into the house she had known a certain fear, a vulnerability, a sadness, but somehow this had become Nick's house, not Grandfather's. Apart from the big change in style, they both had one thing in common, a very confident artistic eye.

'Well?' said Nick, lifting an eyebrow at her.

'I thought this would upset me, Nick.'

'I know you did. Is it my house, Rachael, or are you going to live with your ghosts?'

'Grandfather is still here, don't worry.'

'Exuberant, forceful, a real personality, I'll be pleased to have him. Nonetheless, this is my home now.'

'Yes, I can see that.'

'Do—you—like—it, Rachael?' He drew her to him, spacing out his words.

'Is it important to you, Nick, what I think?'

'I've learned I have to drag things out of you.'

'Then I'm being very mean. My dearest grandfather would congratulate you. He would say you have real style, *character*. Grandfather was a great one for character. I congratulate you too, Nick. The house doesn't make me sad. It's still my friend.'

'You funny child, I think you love the house best of all. Would you marry me for it?'

'Certainly not. It's high time you found a suitable woman.'

'What are you afraid of?'

She was moving swiftly away from him. 'I'm trying to join the party, Nick.'

'Oh, is that all?' he said airily. 'You can be sure they'll all welcome you. Especially my friend Tony.'

164

That, at least, was true. Young men of her own age group sometimes went in awe of Rachael's assurance and beauty, but Nick's bachelor friends had no such inhibitions. She was swept up at once into a crowd of sophisticates and presently found herself enthroned in an armchair surrounded by three of Nick's particular friends, all of them male. Flame-like, with a natural charm of manner, she found she was enjoying herself immensely, her laughing amber eyes more provocative than she meant, her supreme self-confidence stemming mainly from the fact that none of them could mean anything to her. There was only Nick, and he was very busy doing his duty as host, in conversation here, there and everywhere, while Rachael allowed herself the luxury of following him about with her eyes. Every now and again he caught her at this betraying practice and gave her his white, faintly mocking, smile, his glance moving on to the bright, interested faces of his friends, all trained on her.

Tony was easily the most determined of them, and soon he decided he wanted to dance. Rachael found herself out on the terrace where other couples surged around them, relaxed and smiling, the women delectably dressed, counter-attractions to the more sombre dress of the men. Waiters were circling with trays of champagne and other drinks, and after a while Tony broke off to take two glasses, drawing Rachael down to the stone balustrade. He obviously considered himself a connoisseur of beautiful girls, but he was very light-hearted and funny, and good-looking too in a nut-brown way. Rachael kept up the conversation easily, but she could no longer see Nick.

About an hour later, Vanessa arrived with the same party of friends that had joined her at the auction, including Ronald. Rachael recognised them immediately. Vanessa looked perfect in a pewter satin evening shirt with a long claret-coloured satin skirt, a wide silver belt around her slender waist and ropes of pearls and glittering silver chains. Nick went to greet her, and all of the women of the party, Vanessa included, kissed him. Maybe it was a special kind of game, Rachael reasoned. All of them knew the rules, but he did not seem to lavish special time or attention on any one of them, and Ronald, who looked almost as colourful as the women in a kind of evening caftan, had his hand shaken very briefly.

'Ah, there's Van!' Tony said, looking up from the ice cubes at the bottom of his glass. 'Do you know her?'

'Yes, we've met.'

'You don't sound very enthusiastic,' Tony grinned, not beating about the bush himself. 'Come to that, I'm not very enthusiastic either. Can't see what Nick sees in her, though she is very striking.'

'I expect you've heard they're getting married?'

'What?' Tony almost shrieked, his brown eyes snapping. 'That comes as a bit of a shock.'

Rachael immediately felt better. 'Perhaps I shouldn't have mentioned it.'

'Good lord!' Tony said, almost indignantly. 'You'd think Nick would tell me a simple thing like that.'

'How long have you known him?'

'For ever! Since we were kids. Nick was always the cleverest kid in the class and I was always the dumbest

166

until I turned about twelve. Are you sure you've got your research right?'

'Perhaps we'd better forget it. If it's true, no doubt Nick will tell you.'

'I'd say so. I'd just have to be his best man. Tell me, Rachael, what man can afford to ignore his friends? Now, Van, she's a very possessive woman. In fact I think she could, if she wished, insult you. She wouldn't be in the least afraid of snubbing Nick's humble friends. Of course with young Jon, the obvious solution is for Nick to remarry.'

'You must have known Jon's mother?' Rachael asked quietly.

'Yes, I did. Anne was the sweetest possible person. None of us could believe it when she died. It was a tremendous shock to everybody, though poor old Nick bore the secret for a year, even from Anne. She adored him. He must be missing a woman like that from his life. But Vanessa now ... she seems to lack something vital. Warmth, I'd call it, but who knows, she might be very different with Nick. She's probably got her good qualities and she can be very agreeable when she likes. But don't let's waste time talking about Van. Let's dance.' Tony started to his feet, grasping her arm. 'Here comes McGuire, but I saw you first. Are you interested in sailing? I have a superb little boat and there's the whole of the harbour at our disposal!'

Rachael had to agree that she liked sailing, but she didn't want to commit herself. Brett often took her out on his father's boat. They lived right on the blue sparkling harbour with their own boat shed and slipway. Tony was getting fairly insistent, and it was quite obvious that he was taken with her. His friend Jake McGuire was at that moment complaining to Nick about certain persons monopolising Nick's youngest and best-looking guest. Nick listened to him with strict impartiality, then decided it was the host's job to do that. He turned and made his way out on to the terrace, stopping here and there at some laughing group.

Floating past them on the terrace, Rachael heard a woman say:

'Why, Van must be the luckiest woman in the world.'

Tony's teasing voice became immediately serious. 'Did you hear that?'

'What does it mean?' asked Rachael.

Tony followed the woman's progress with his eyes. 'That's a friend of Van's. Could be she heard the same news you did. And to think I grew up with Nick!'

'I don't think I can get over it myself.'

'Here's Nick now ..: Listen, old son!'

'No, you listen!' Nick said humorously. 'This is my party and I'm dancing with Rachael.'

'Anything you say. Would you like me to go home?'

'No, it's all right. Go and see Jake, he's ready to push you off the roof.'

'Just because he can't hold Rachael's hand?'

'Something like that. Go on, Tony, move.'

'Why, bless your little heart, of course I will. Aren't I your friend? Coming with me tomorrow, Rachael?'

'Yes, thank you, Tony, I will.' Rachael smiled at him, only at that moment deciding any such thing. If Nick excelled at double-dealing she could play her own game.

'And what does that mean?' Nick asked her, taking her smoothly into his arms.

'Tony asked me out in his boat.'

'What a thrill! One of you will end up sour, possibly both. Tony's always having engine trouble.'

'You sound jealous.'

'Whisper it, Rachael.'

'How come you've left Vanessa alone?' she asked.

'Is she alone?' he asked in a ruminative voice. 'I thought blessed Ronald was with her.'

'They have similar expressions.'

'So I've noticed.'

She looked away from him, her amber eyes glittery. 'Gran is thinking of going overseas for six months.'

He pulled back a little, staring down at her. 'Is she up to it, the travelling? She'll be heading into the winter.'

'The cold doesn't bother her. I'm thinking of going as well.'

His face seemed to tauten. 'When was all this decided?'

'Tonight, as a matter of fact. I've never travelled, you know. I'm looking forward to it.'

'You don't sound very cheerful. In fact I can feel the tension in you. What on earth's the matter now?'

'There you go again, Nick,' she said jerkily. 'We'll never resolve our little differences.'

'Let's just say the only way to stop you is to kiss you thoroughly.'

'That would be extremely unwise,' she said, feeling utterly distracted.

'It's a miracle to find you two minutes the same. You

169

look as if you were sent to earth to dazzle men, not incite them to strangle you.'

'That sounds delightful! You can't mean it, Nick?'

'I seem to be slipping from my civilised stand. Yes, I do.'

'Why, I thought you'd be more impassive than anybody. I was very impressed with you the day I saw you in court.'

'And you stuck out a mile with those blatant black curls.'

'I thought I looked rather gorgeous.'

'You're unhappy. Can't you tell me why?'

Immediately she lowered her thick eyelashes. Nick just went on holding her in complete silence. Neither of them said a word, but something elemental was pulsing between them. A funny little shiver ran down Rachael's spine. Impulsively she moved closer to him, murmuring his name. He *must* know how she felt, for all her silly antagonism. She seemed to be locked in his arms unable to break free, the two of them moving in the sweetest, most natural rhythm. If she looked up at him now, her eyes would tell him she loved him. So there was no one but the two of them and she wished them to stay that way for ever.

'Rachael?'

Was he going to tell her now she was only a stupid child? It wouldn't come easily, because he was very kind, much kinder than she had ever expected. She felt a terrible ache of sadness.

'Don't say it, Nick.'

'Are you sure you know what I was going to say?

Your skin is like satin.' His hand moved lightly down her back.

'*Please!*' There was a kind of pleading in her voice.

Almost as if she had prayed for deliverance, Jake McGuire came to claim his dance, saying he had waited quite long enough.

'End of your dance, Nick, I think. The duties of a host and all that!'

'I know how it is.' Nick relinquished her, smiling in mock defeat. 'Jake's an architect, Rachael. You know, he figures out plans and how to build things.'

'But I don't have your succeess!' Jake maintained.

'Didn't I work for it?'

'You did, boy!' Jake said emphatically.

'Well then.' Nick walked away from them, very urbane and elegant, and Jake turned to look down into Rachael's creamy face.

'Nick followed his father's footsteps into law and I took up architecture to settle a family argument. Mother wanted me to be a doctor, every family needs one, and Dad wanted me to go into the business.'

'Which is?'

'Building boats. That's how I met Tony. He launched me into Nick's charmed circle and am I grateful! Nick really knows how to live. What a fabulous place!'

'Yes,' Rachael answered. Nick was now dancing with Vanessa, who for once looked surprisingly alive as if his blue gaze dusted her with diamonds. Jake talked all the while, but Rachael scarcely heard him. Nick looked just as attractive, just as attentive, dancing with any woman. Probably he made them all feel the same way. It was a gift, sexual magnetism, and he had it in plenty. She felt as though the evening was ending instead of hardly beginning. She had two options open to her, to wilt like so much crumpled tissue paper or to glitter. Pride made her decide on the latter.

From then on she seemed to be spinning non-stop, the centre of a bright, ever-changing circle. Only one group failed to surge around her, Vanessa and company, though they followed her vivacious progress with tight disapproving glances and numerous sotto voce comments. Sometimes a mercurial temperament came in handy. Rachael was giving the performance of her life. No one could have guessed what she felt inside, it was simply that she wasn't going to quit the field without her colours flying. Nick's friends evidently found her dazzling, for she received more invitations in one evening than she had ever collected in a dozen weeks. She knew that when it was all over, she would have a violent headache.

Supper was sumptuous. She had it with Tony, who was barely able to hold his attraction in check. Previously he had thought young girls a crashing bore, but Rachael seemed to be extremely poised and witty. He supposed it was her upbringing. It had taken him half the evening to find out she was *that* Ross girl. Nick hadn't breathed a word to him about Rachael's background. That then explained it. Her grandfather had been one of the city's most colourful personalities for many long years.

Rachael managed to hold Nick at bay, every time he came near her, but once when she was telling a few of his friends about the wondrous trip she was intending, he interjected quite clearly that it would 'do her the world of good!' Nothing could be plainer. He simply didn't care one way or the other. She wasn't the only woman interested in Nick. Neither was Vanessa. More than half the women at the party seemed to be throwing themselves at him. Good looks coupled with money threw nine out of ten women into a silly, gushing flutter. It certainly put things into perspective for her. How easy it was for one to delude oneself, to read everything into nothing. She might be too impressionable, but her feelings ran deep.

By the end of the evening she was exhausted and she couldn't put Nick off once more. She was astonished in any case by her own fearlessness, in fact she was near to tears after an evening of acting as if she had come straight from fairyland. Only Nick's hand locking her wrist was reality.

'I brought you and I'm going to take you home again,' he said with no hint of gallantry or pleasure.

'I can easily walk!' she said with some spirit. 'In any case, Tony has already asked me.'

'Tony has just been blinded by your excessive good looks. He doesn't really know you.'

'Surely he can be allowed to change that?'

'Not tonight, anyway!'

'Then this seems the moment to die. You're angry!'

'No, not really. It's just when I start something, I always finish it.'

'You're making me look conspicuous!' she accused him. Vanessa was at that moment staring at her with absolute venom.

'Poor child!' he murmured in a smooth, taunting

voice. 'Could it be true you believe it? I mean, after such an extravagant evening. Most of them have gone off thinking you a sensation. Your grandfather would have been proud of you.'

She stared up at him, her topaz eyes brilliant. 'Oh no, you're striking the wrong note. *You're* the sensation. You could wreck any number of lives.'

'Be still!' he stopped her, by pressing her hand, 'or I just won't be responsible for the consequences.'

The last of the guests were leaving, making drowsy contented exclamations, Tony disappointed but bearing up well, the women touching their lips to Nick's cheek, the men pumping his hand. There were snatches of renewed invitations, a painfully frosty 'Goodnight!' from Vanessa to Rachael, though she held her body close to Nick, promising to see him tomorrow. At last it was all over.

'How charming!' Rachael said. 'But shouldn't you have taken Vanessa home?'

'She has her own car.'

'Ah well! you'll see her tomorrow.'

'It would seem so.'

'You don't sound awfully sorry about it. The house looks beautiful,' she said, swirling around, her skirt flying.

'Yes, it does. Come along, Rachael. I'd better take you home.'

'I could have gone by myself,' she told him airily.

'You're so wrong.'

'I'm quite capable of it.'

'Come with me, Rachael, it's your only chance.'

Nick held out his hand and she smiled at him, as

174

though she had only just then decided to surrender. 'All right, I will.'

'We'll walk.'

'I shouldn't risk it, with *you*!'

'You will.'

'Don't feel sorry for me, Nick Retford!' she warned him, catching his sparkling mocking glance. 'I'm going round the world.'

'You owe it to yourself, Rachael.'

'I do?'

'You sound uncertain. Are you sure you want to go?' He looked down at her dreamy, confused face. 'Come on, I shouldn't keep you out of your bed.' He pulled her out through the front door and shut it after them.

'I've got to be free, Nick!' she protested. 'It's just something that has to be done.'

'You have to decide that, Rachael. *I* can't. I must admit you could spend a little time growing up.'

'Oh, *thank* you!' she said with emphasis. 'You certainly know how to put me in my place.'

'The trouble is you won't stay there.'

It was useless to protest that she really was a woman. The night sky was perfect, studded with stars, and she looked up at it with a mixture of delight and sadness. The Lodge seemed awfully far away, the garden an enormous scented jungle, the tunnel under the interlacing trees of the drive as black as ebony. Night was a new element with its own powerful excitement. The breeze fanned her flushed cheeks.

'Can I ask you one question, Nick?'

'As long as it's not too personal.'

'Are you really getting married in the New Year?'

'Yes.' He said it with terrible, direct cruelty, probably meaning to be kind.

'Then I don't think you're a very honourable man,' she informed him.

His hands at her waist were firm to the point of hardness. 'You're the first one to doubt it.'

'Did you kiss me by accident?' she asked, with frightening intensity.

His low laugh infuriated her. 'Rachael, you're priceless!'

'Then for what reason did you do it? I'm not so stupid I can't learn something from it.'

'Some things are inevitable, Rachael.'

'That's not an acceptable answer.' Furiously she broke away from him, her flying feet scarcely seeming to touch the ground. She ran lightly, swiftly, a natural sprinter. The lights of the Lodge flashed out through the trees. This was her home ground. Here she was the expert. She knew every inch of it. She could lose him. Her long skirt fluttered and whipped around her, her hair tossed into a riot of curls. He would be angry for a while, but he deserved it. It was monstrous the way he treated her, though perhaps he thought he was completing her education.

She ran straight into his arms with wide, shining eyes, astonished that he had somehow got there before her. She was beaten. His arm went around her, crushing her to him, his hand came out to brush her hair away from her face.

'Don't you dare!' she said, still angry, but his caressing hand round her throat almost stopped her. 'Please, Nick.' An upsurge of excitement made her voice shaky.

176

'Surely I won?' His hand clasped her nape, shaping it, her hair curling over the cuff of his jacket. 'Anyway, I enjoyed it.'

'This is unfair—unfair advantage.'

'Hmm, but it's irresistible.'

It was impossible to twist away from him, so she gave up the fight, her body of its own accord searching for comfort. She loved him desperately, and unconsciously her whole being was projecting her desires. It was too much for him. He claimed her mouth with such urgency that it had a kind of desperation about it as if he intended never to kiss her again. She locked her arms tightly around his neck, neither of them gentle with the other. There was too much emotion to be compressed into this very short time. Her own response, she knew, was reckless and impassioned and without reservation. But what was the good of it? Surely he knew she loved him. In another minute she could deny him nothing.

It was Nick who drew back, pulling her arms down though he must have known he was humiliating her. 'Don't say it!' she put her fingers across his mouth. 'I know. Extreme provocation. It won't happen again.'

She was still trembling with excitement and the fear of giving away her most closely guarded secret. The physical communication between them was shattering, but she was correct in thinking a man didn't always marry the woman who filled that particular role. There were other more prosaic considerations. Vanessa was a different kind of woman again. She tried not to think about her, but she couldn't allow herself to dream on. Maggie, that strong personality, had come to her res-

177

cue offering a distraction, though it wasn't until after ten the next morning, waiting for Tony to arrive, when she saw Vanessa's Volvo sweep up the drive, that she finally decided to do something constructive about her future.

She would see the rest of the world. Valuable lessons were most often painful. She was young. She would survive—*somehow*. It had been worth it at that. She had lost her head, but now it was all over. Probably Nick would breathe a sigh of relief. Their attraction, though mutual, was evidently unsuitable. A world trip was merciful. She had known from the very first moment that Nick was dangerous to her. Now she had to cultivate the great gift of forgetfulness. In time she might earn a measure of success, or was it her destiny to know terrible disappointments?

CHAPTER EIGHT

IT was almost closing time when Rachael made her way out on to the street, laden with parcels and boxes she realised she should have had sent, but the car wasn't too far away in the city parking lot. The late edition of the newspapers had hit the stands and her eyes automatically ran down the red printed poster of the STOP PRESS.

CITY DRAMA
YOUTH GOES BERSERK
LEADING BARRISTER KNIFED

She knew, as she struggled frantically for some small change, that it was Nick. Nothing else could account for the icy feeling around her heart. She was sick to the point of fainting. There were no pictures, only a brief account. The incident had taken place outside the Courts. It was established that the premeditated and vicious attack had not been directed at Mr Dominic Retford, Q.C. as first thought, but Inspector George Lennox who had been walking with him. It was understood the youth had recently been detained in a psychiatric hospital, and witnesses confirmed from the youth's frenzied shouting that he had intended serious bodily harm to the Inspector. Mr Retford's alertness and presentiment of danger had averted a possible tragedy. Inspector Lennox had been shaken by the incident but not harmed. Mr Retford had been treated at St Vincent's Hospital for slashes to his right arm and shoulder from a flick knife and allowed to go home. His injuries had been sustained while overpowering the youth, who had been taken into custody and who would appear in the Magistrates' Court in the morning.

Rachael stood in the busy street, all her plans toppling around her. To her dismay she felt like bursting into tears. She couldn't stand it until she saw Nick herself. Jon, so close to his father, would be frightened and shocked. She would have to hurry back to him. Her feelings for Nick went too deep to worry about whether they were on speaking terms or not. She was far too frantic. It was almost as if his assailant had slashed at her, cutting her arm and her dress.

She ran to the car park, her heart pounding, her pallor pronounced. This could have been murder and it frightened her. There she had been for most of the day trying to buy warm clothing in the middle of summer, now *this*! It shocked and scared her. Jon would need her. He was a small boy, after all, even though he was a gallant little fellow. Mrs Stevenson would be there to comfort him, but they all knew Rachael and Jon were special friends and they saw one another every day. It was useless for her to tell herself Nick mightn't want to see her. She had to see *him*, otherwise she would have no peace at all.

Once in the car, Rachael struggled to get complete control of herself. The traffic was heavy. It was no time to let her mind wander. Once on the highway she put her foot down, reaching the limit. The sunlight bounced off the hood of the Mercedes. Behind her tightly controlled face was turmoil. She kept seeing Nick in danger. His image blotted out everything. She had seldom covered the distance in such a short time. She swung through the gates and continued on up the winding drive to the main house, parking the car near the tall banks of hydrangeas. Blue like Nick's eyes.

She stood still for a moment, staring up at the open front door, then she ran up the short flight of steps, for once blind to the beauty of the house. Nick took precedence over everything in her mind. Jon flew for her like a small wild creature, burying his head in her skirt.

'Darling!' Her heart twisted in her. Was the danger more real than she thought? Her own voice seemed to be coming from a distance. She looked down at the child, smoothing his hair with her hand. 'Where's Daddy?'

Jon's voice rose shrilly. 'He's been stabbed! Someone tried to kill him.'

'No, no,' she said in distress. 'He's all right.'

'It isn't a secret, Rachael, it's in all the papers.'

'Miss Ross!' Mrs Stevenson stood in the doorway.

'Where's Mr Retford?' demanded Rachael.

'He's coming home. He's all right. I've tried to tell Jon, but one of his little friends got the story all wrong.'

'There!' Rachael said to the child. 'Does that convince you?'

'Nothing will convince me until I see Dad,' Jon answered, quite obviously frightened. 'Stay with me, Rachael.'

'Of course I will.'

'Does my grandmother know?' Rachael turned her head to speak to Nick's housekeeper.

'Yes. She rang the house. She was very upset. Naturally I rang back immediately Mr Retford contacted me himself. He sounded just the same.'

'Let's sit on the front steps, Rachael, and wait. I feel sick,' said Jon.

'Listen, darling, Daddy was very brave. He saved the other man's life and he rang to let you know he was safe and sound.'

'I just want him to come home,' Jon said doggedly. 'I wouldn't know what to do without him.'

'Neither would I.'

'You mean you care about him like I do?' Jon asked with no surprise.

'Of course I do.' Rachael's topaz eyes sparkled with tears and she blinked them away. 'Here, sit beside me. Daddy's perfectly safe and soon he'll be coming home to you.'

She called back to Mrs Stevenson. 'Would you mind ringing the Lodge, Mrs Stevenson? Tell my grandmother I'm waiting up here with Jon.'

'I'll do that for you, Miss Ross. It's very kind of you to come up,' Mrs Stevenson said gratefully. 'It's the first time I haven't been able to do a thing with Jon. He's been obsessed with the idea his father had been seriously injured. I felt sick with fright myself until I heard his calm voice.'

When Nick got home fifteen minutes later, he saw Rachael sitting with his son, both of them so pale and fragile, each with a comforting arm around the other.

For a moment they seemed to him two children who had been brutally shocked, but at the first sight of him standing quite steadily outside the car their faces broke into expressions of blessed relief. Rachael stood up and Jon raced like a hare down the marble steps.

'Dad, you're all right!'

'Large as life.' Nick hugged his son, across the intervening space meeting Rachael's golden gaze. Her pride fell into dust. She even managed to laugh.

'Oh, Nick, what a bad time you've given us!'

He reached her, his arm wound around Jon, touching her cheek, his blue eyes filled with the most profound tenderness, whether for his son or her or both of them she didn't know. 'I suppose you read the story in the papers?'

'Yes. I was in town. Jon heard it at his friend's place.'

'That was bad. I might have known you'd rush to comfort him.'

Mrs Stevenson came to the top of the steps and he smiled at her. 'All in one piece, Stevie!'

'Oh, Mr Retford!' She was obviously trying not to cry.

'I'll change my shirt, if you don't mind.'

'I'll lay one out for you.' She bustled away, anxious to do something. He was still wearing his jacket and she could imagine what state his pale blue shirt was in. Jon and Miss Rachael were clinging to him like two children so recently desolate they still couldn't get their colour back.

Nick looked down at the girl beside him. 'I've never seen you so pale. You look like a beautiful waif.'

'Rachael loves you just as much as I do!' Jon said

183

with the unthinking ardour of a child. 'We were worrying frightfully.'

'Do you, Rachael?'

She looked back at him, gone beyond all pretending. 'Yes, I do. Try living with that one, Nick Retford!'

'Then how are you going to account for taking that world trip?'

'I thought you wanted me to go?'

He shrugged his injured shoulder. 'Let's go inside so you two can sit quietly. I've never seen such a pair of white faces. I'll have a quick shower and change my clothes—I've got the hospital all over me.'

'Can I come with you, Dad?'

'No, you stay here and keep Rachael company. You'll stay for dinner, won't you, Rachael? We'll have it early. One way or the other I missed out on lunch.'

'You will, won't you, Rachael?' Jon asked, visibly brightening.

'Yes, of course I will. Let's go and ring Gran. You can speak to her and tell her your father is safely home again. She'll be pleased.'

Nick smiled at them and gave them a solemn bow; then he walked up the stairway, leaving them with a rage of love and relief in their hearts.

The whole evening the three of them spent together, but Rachael could only guess at Nick's thoughts. She went up with Jon when it was time for bed and re-arranged his pillows, then she bent and kissed his wide forehead.

'Sleep well, young man.'

'Isn't it funny, I'm tired out. 'Night, Rachael, and thanks for caring about Dad.'

Rachael laughed. 'You know perfectly well you can include yourself, but remember your father has lots of ardent admirers. I'm just Rachael, not old enough to be wise!'

'Don't give up!' Jon opened his eyes to say surprisingly.

Downstairs again Rachael felt bothered by extreme shyness. She had given her heart away, but she couldn't brood about it. She had experienced a great deal that day. The fact was she had loved Nick right from the beginning and hadn't known it. She entered the living-room quietly, but Nick wasn't there. She moved outside on to the terrace where the breeze carried the scent of the flowers. Then she saw him. He was leaning against the balustrade, his head turned towards her.

'What are you doing?' she asked.

'Waiting for you.'

A flame of wonder overcame her. His blue eyes seemed to be offering her ecstasy. She made a funny little articulate sound and ran towards him, encircling his tall frame with her two arms, trying to avoid his bandaged arm and shoulder. 'Just being with you is a pleasure beyond enduring,' she said, and laid her head against his chest. 'I'm not hurting you, am I?'

'Don't be silly. You couldn't hurt me *this* way. Rachael?' He grasped a handful of her hair and tipped her head back, searching her eyes. 'There's only one thing that might get me down. You're not going on this trip, are you?'

'Possibly.'

'I won't let you, though I know I'm being damned selfish! By the way, I am not going to marry Vanessa, as you seem to have been spreading around.'

'Not *me*, Mr Retford, though I thought she'd make you an ideal wife.'

'Haven't you noticed I happen to love someone quite different? *Very* different, in fact!'

'Is it me after all?'

'Brilliant, the way you express yourself. Yes, it's you, Rachael. Before all.'

'Are you sure you're not looking for the right step-mother for Jon?'

'I'm thinking of myself. As it happens Jon will benefit as well.'

'Then why have you been giving me all these head-aches?'

'Forgive me.' He looked down into her eyes, challenging her a little. 'Perhaps I thought you should suffer a bit!'

'You brute!'

'Close your eyes. Sometimes I think you're the only woman I've ever known.'

'How do you know I'm not marrying you for the Swan?' she whispered.

'I'm much too clever for you. Besides, I haven't asked you yet.'

'Ask me now.'

'Marry me, Rachael,' he said in a voice she had never quite heard from him before. 'Nothing less will satisfy me and it has to be soon.'

'I think it would be the best thing,' she murmured, looking so beautiful and vital that he had to restrain himself from picking her up there and then and making her part of him. Instead he took her glowing face into his finely shaped hands and lowered his head.

'I pledge you anything you want!'

'Just kiss me. I don't want one empty space left in me for doubt!'

Inside, the phone had to ring insistently to part them.

Rachael drew back, smoothing her tumbled hair. 'You'd better answer it!' she stammered softly, still disorientated from the touch of his mouth.

'No, *you*,' he smiled at her. 'It's your house as well as mine.'

There was a little silence between them and she looked at him, loving him. 'Absurd I ever fought you.'

'Yes. Now you're bound to me with a thousand chains.'

'It's all I want!'

She turned and ran into the house to answer her grandmother. Miracles did happen at Swans' Reach, and her grandmother didn't even catch her breath.

Other titles you will enjoy by
MARGARET WAY
in the Mills & Boon Romance Series

For details of how to obtain the titles listed above please
turn to page 191.

Also available this month
Four titles in our Mills & Boon Classics Series

Specially chosen reissues of the best in Romantic Fiction
March's titles are:

HEART OF A ROSE *by Rachel Lindsay*
Rose was just an ordinary hard-working girl who had been
lucky enough to land a job as florist in the glamorous South
of France. She had no opinion at all of the rich, idle playboy
Lance Hammond – when she gave him any thought at all,
that is. Certainly she had no idea of the far-reaching effect
he was soon to have on her life.

MASTER OF FALCON'S HEAD *by Anne Mather*
It was seven years since Tamar had left Falcon's Wherry,
her heart broken and her life in ruins. Now she was back –
and her feelings for the man who had done it all were as deep
as ever. But hadn't too much happened for either of them to
turn the clock back?

OPPORTUNE MARRIAGE *by Kay Thorpe*
Lisa admitted that she had married Brad to solve a problem
of her own – but she had thought that she also attracted him.
How was the marriage likely to work out when she discovered
that his motives for it had been as calculated as her own?

THE MAN IN COMMAND *by Anne Weale*
Sanchia had willingly taken responsibility for the orphaned
Rowland children – but that was before she realized that
their uncle Tom Bartlett, in his turn, had apparently decided
to take responsibility for her!

Mills & Boon Classics – all that's great in Romantic Reading!

BUY THEM TODAY only 40p

April Paperbacks

AEGEAN QUEST *by Elizabeth Ashton*
Who *was* Nikolaos Paleologus, Priscilla demanded, to say
that her sister couldn't marry his brother? She'd soon see
about that!

TWO PINS IN A FOUNTAIN *by Jane Arbor*
Although Paula had fallen in love with Gratien de Tourcy,
her love was plainly one-sided . . .

A MATTER OF CHANCE *by Betty Neels*
Cressida's employer was kind and friendly, but she couldn't
say the same for his partner, Giles van der Teile!

THE VILLA FAUSTINO *by Katrina Britt*
Joanna longed to visit London – but how could she leave
Ramon?

GOBLIN HILL *by Essie Summers*
Gareth Morgan couldn't forget the old family scandal – or
forgive Faith for it!

THE RIVER LORD *by Kay Thorpe*
All Keely wanted was to go on the Amazon expedition to find
the Fire Flower, but Greg Stirling refused to take her.
Would he change his mind?

A MAN OF IMPORTANCE *by Anne Hampson*
Taran's legacy had some unexpected snags – and the
biggest of all was the autocratic Armand de Courtenay.

BOUND FOR MARANDOO *by Kerry Allyne*
Jade was joking when she said she wanted a husband, but
unfortunately Tory believed her . . .

DEVIL'S GATEWAY *by Yvonne Whittal*
Her new home seemed sinister to Vicky, and so did the
near-stranger who was her husband . . .

WINDS FROM THE SEA *by Margaret Pargeter*
Sara went to the Hebrides because she wanted a change from
city life. Certainly Hugh Fraser was different from the men
she was used to!

35p net each
Available April 1977

Your Mills & Boon Classics Selection!

☐ C1
THE TIME IS SHORT
Nerina Hilliard

☐ C2
PRICE OF LOVE
Rachel Lindsay

☐ C3
THEY CAME TO VALEIRA
Rosalind Brett

☐ C4
THE PRIMROSE BRIDE
Kathryn Blair

☐ C5
TREVALLION
Sara Seale

☐ C6
THE SEA WAIF
Anne Weale

☐ C7
LOVE THIS STRANGER
Rosalind Brett

☐ C8
THREE WOMEN
Celine Conway

☐ C9
THE SCARS SHALL FADE
Nerina Hilliard

☐ C10
NEVER TO LOVE
Anne Weale

☐ C11
WINDS OF ENCHANTMENT
Rosalind Brett

☐ C12
CHILD FRIDAY
Sara Seale

☐ C 13
LOVE AND LUCY GRANGER
Rachel Lindsay

☐ C14
FLOWER FOR A BRIDE
Barbara Rowan

☐ C15
UNDER THE STARS OF PARIS
Mary Burchell

☐ C16
TO CATCH A UNICORN
Sara Seale

☐ C17
AND NO REGRETS
Rosalind Brett

☐ C18
MAYENGA FARM
Kathryn Blair

☐ C19
BRITTLE BONDAGE
Rosalind Brett

☐ C20
HOUSE OF LORRAINE
Rachel Lindsay

☐ C21
HOUSE IN THE TIMBERWOODS
Joyce Dingwell

☐ C22
FLOWER OF THE MORNING
Celine Conway

☐ C23
BARBARY MOON
Kathryn Blair

☐ C24
THE ENGLISH TUTOR
Sara Seale

☐ C25
SPRING AT THE VILLA
Rosalind Brett

☐ C26
THE HOUSE BY THE LAKE
Eleanor Farnes

☐ C27
THE GIRL AT SNOWY RIVER
Joyce Dingwell

☐ C28
DANGEROUS KIND OF LOVE
Kathryn Blair

☐ C29
THE HOUSE OF ADRIANO
Nerina Hilliard

☐ C30
FLOWER IN THE WIND
Celine Conway

All priced at 35p. Please tick your requirements and use
the handy order form overleaf.